SODOR

SODOR

# THOMAS & FRIENDS™

# STORY TIME COLLECTION

Thomas the Tank Engine & Friends™

CREATED BY BRITT ALLCROFT

Based on the Railway Series by The Reverend W Awdry.
 Published in the United States by Random House Children's Books, a division of Random House LLC, 1745 Broadway, New York, NY 10019, and in Canada by Random House of Canada Limited, Toronto, Penguin Random House Companies. Random House and the colophon are registered trademarks of Random House LLC.

Visit us on the Web!
randomhouse.com/kids
www.thomasandfriends.com
Teachers and librarians, for a variety of teaching tools, visit us at RHTeachersLibrarians.com
ISBN 978-0-553-49678-9
MANUFACTURED IN CHINA
10 9
Random House Children's Books supports the First Amendment and celebrates the right to read.

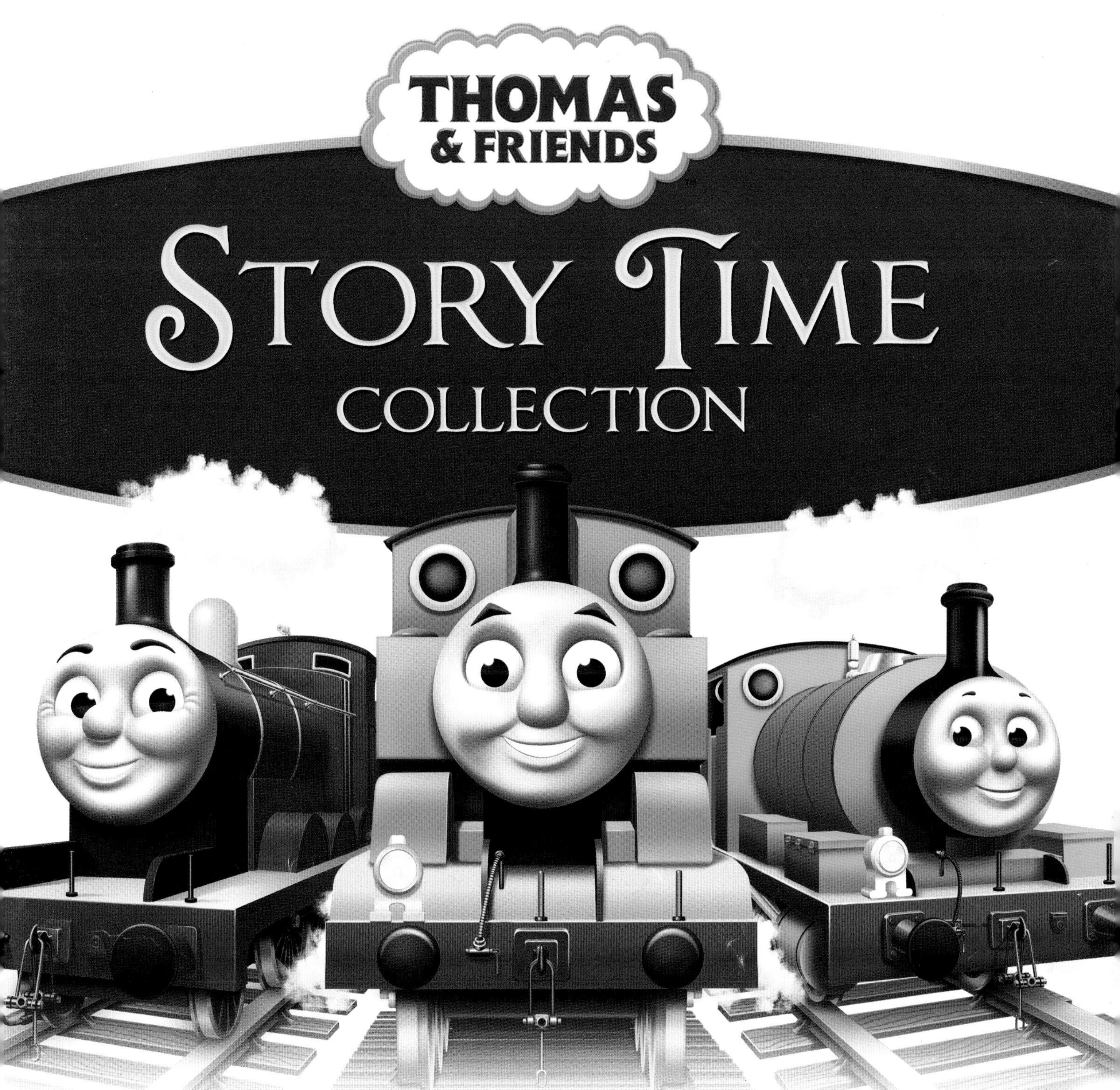


Based on the Railway Series by The Reverend W Awdry

Random House  New York

# Contents

6

SPLATTER

# Little Engines Can Do BIG Things

By Britt Allcroft
Based on The Railway Series by The Reverend W Awdry
Illustrated by Coatimundi Studios

Things were very busy on the Island of Sodor. Sir Topham Hatt was away on vacation, and all the engines were doing their best to be Really Useful.

But Thomas the Tank Engine did not feel useful at all.

3 2
1
1

James teased Thomas for bumping into the buffers.
Gordon scolded Thomas for being late.
They made Thomas feel unimportant.

"Important is big," Gordon told Thomas. "And we are big engines. *You* are small."

"Bossy sprockets!" grumbled Thomas. "I'll show them."

"Little engines *can* do big things," Thomas said to himself. "Especially when they have nice blue paint like me."

But just then Harold the Helicopter flew by, making a cloud of dust. Thomas' nice blue paint got all dirty.

Two nasty diesels made fun of Thomas.
"Let's start laughing now!" they said. And they did.

Thomas was determined to prove that little engines could be Really Useful, too. That night, Thomas was Right on Time doing his mail route.

He even comforted Percy, who felt bad for being late.

The next morning, Thomas saw Henry looking glum.
"Morning, Henry," peeped Thomas. "What's the matter?"
"I've got boiler ache," Henry told him.

Thomas offered to fetch some special coal for Henry.

"Thank you, Thomas," said Henry. "Special coal will make me feel much better."

Thomas smiled and puffed away, feeling Really Useful indeed.

Near a set of old buffers, Thomas set to work collecting the coal cars. But the last car was not coupled properly.

Thomas didn't notice the coal car sliding quietly backward. He didn't notice it mysteriously disappearing through the old buffers. It wasn't until later that Thomas realized the coal car was missing.

"I was up near the buffers when the last coal car disappeared," Thomas told Percy.

Percy got very excited. "Maybe those buffers are the entrance to the Magic Railroad!" he cried.

The engines had heard the legend of the Magic Railroad and of the beautiful golden engine called Lady, who gave the railroad its magic power. Lady had disappeared long ago, and the Magic Railroad had disappeared with her.

"Percy, you are clever!" Thomas exclaimed, and hurried away.

Thomas steamed back to the old buffers. He knew that bringing Lady back would be Really Useful. But he was nervous, too.

"What if I go on the Magic Railroad and my wheels don't work?" thought Thomas. "What if it's dark?"

But Thomas kept going.
He reached the old buffers . . . and passed right through!

The Magic Railroad was dark and scary, but it was also beautiful. Thomas found the missing coal car. With the car coupled properly, he continued along the Magic Railroad.

Thomas passed through another set of buffers and into a world he had never seen before. This was the other end of the Magic Railroad and the home of Lady the Golden Engine.

Lady had not run in many years. But with the help of the special coal from the Island of Sodor, she was soon steaming again.

As Lady moved along, her lovely, happy face was revealed once more. The rails became clear and golden, and beautiful shavings fell behind her and gathered between the tracks.

The Magic Railroad was coming back to life!

Thomas followed Lady back through the buffers.
With a roar, the two little engines burst onto the Island of Sodor.

"Hooray for Thomas!" the engines cheered.
Lady was back, and the Magic Railroad would run once again.
"You see?" said Thomas. "Little engines *can* do big things."

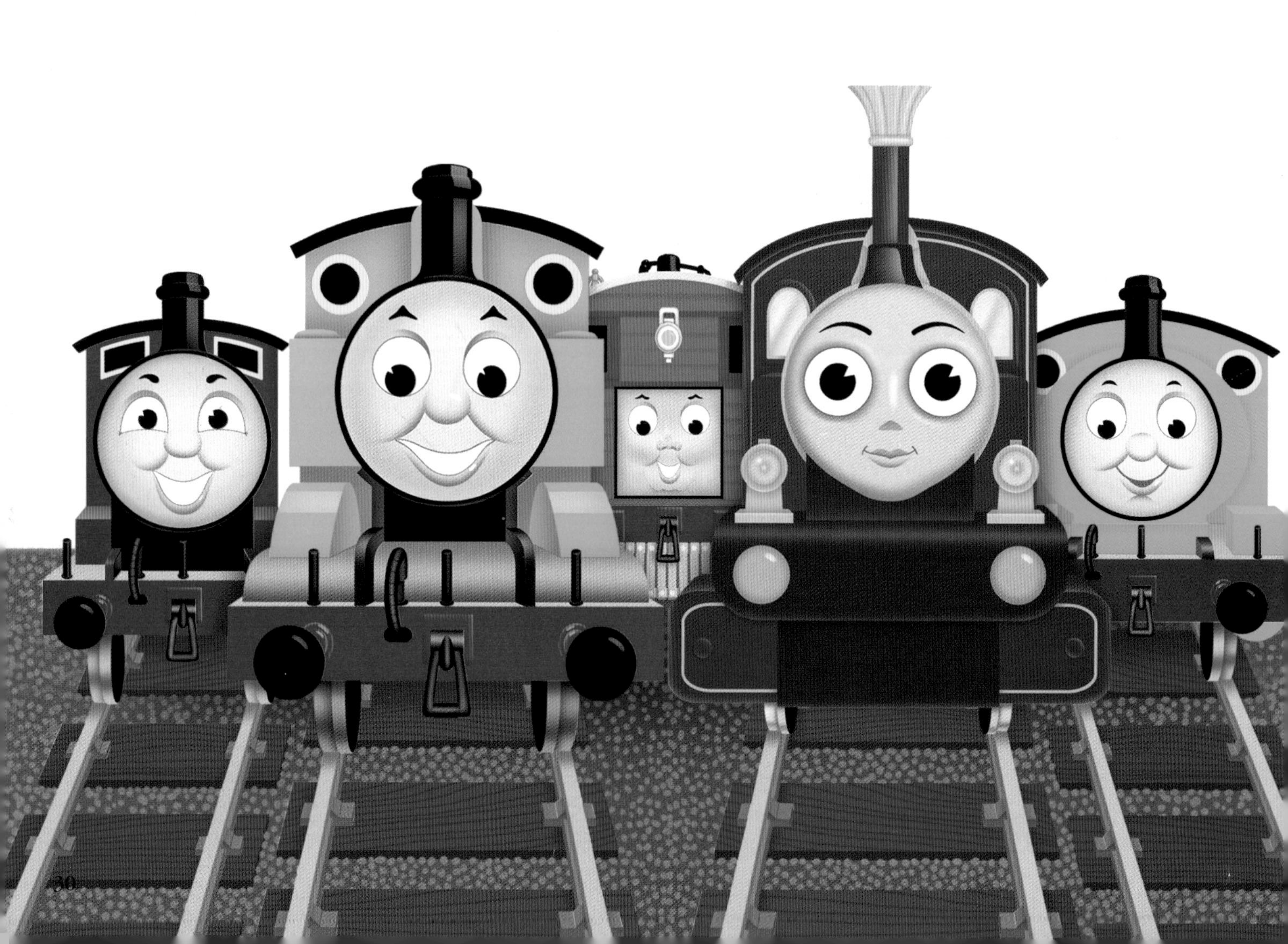

Based on The Railway Series by The Reverend W Awdry
Illustrated by Richard Courtney

CRANKY
URGENT
BULSTRODE

Cranky was unloading a box for Sir Topham Hatt. The box was marked URGENT.

"Humpf," creaked Cranky. "What's so *urgent* about this package?"

Thomas heard Cranky's question.

"If it says *urgent,* we should get it to Sir Topham Hatt as fast as we can!" he said. "I'll take it!"

CRANKY

Just then, Gordon pulled up next to Thomas.

"An *urgent* package needs a speedy train," said Gordon. "I'm the fastest train here, so *I* will have to take the package."

Gordon took the package and set off immediately.

Thomas was left behind. "*I* could have gotten it there quickly," he peeped.

Gordon hurried down the track and took a hilly shortcut. Suddenly, he saw a red signal. Some rocks had fallen across his path. He was stuck!

Just then, Toby came by on an open track.

"Help!" said Gordon. "I have an *urgent* package for Sir Topham Hatt."

"I can take it down the hill," said Toby.

"Thank you!" Gordon called as Toby chugged away.

Toby clickety-clacked quickly down the hill.

Percy was waiting at the bottom.

"Thank you for bringing the *urgent* package down," said Percy. "Now I can take it to Sir Topham Hatt."

"Sir Topham Hatt will be very proud of me," Percy tooted as he hurried along.

Percy rounded a bend and saw James ahead of him pulling two Troublesome Trucks. James was going very slowly because the trucks had their brakes on.

"*We* want to take the package," said the Troublesome Trucks. "We won't release our brakes until you give it to us."

Percy was very mad, but he knew that the *urgent* package had to get to Sir Topham Hatt quickly. With a sigh, he gave it to the trucks.

"No more trouble from you trucks," said James. The trucks released their brakes. James and the trucks quickly left Percy behind.

James was glad that he would be the one to deliver this *urgent* package now.

James was going so fast he almost didn't see . . .

. . . the broken track!

"Oh, no!" wailed James. "Now Sir Topham Hatt will never get his *urgent* package."

"I'll take the *urgent* package," said Harold, landing next to James. He took the package and flew off.

HAROLD

Harold soared over the countryside. He looked down and saw Thomas pulling into Tidmouth Station.

Thomas had been faster than Gordon after all!

"Where's my package?" Sir Topham Hatt asked.

Just then, Harold landed. "I have it, Sir," he said. Then he told Thomas and Sir Topham Hatt what had happened.

Finally, Sir Topham Hatt opened the *urgent* package. What could be inside?

It's a shiny new hat!

"Just in time for tonight's big party," Sir Topham Hatt said, putting the hat on his head. "And, Thomas, next time there is an *urgent* package . . ."

"... I want *you* to bring it!"

# Down at the Docks

Based on The Railway Series by The Reverend W Awdry
Illustrated by Richard Courtney

CRANKY
BULSTRODE
5

**P***eeeeep! Everyone sure looks busy today,* thought Thomas. He was on the hill overlooking the Brendam Docks. From above the busy harbor, Thomas could look down and see all of the other engines working hard.

"Maybe I can do something to help." And down he went.

When Thomas arrived at the docks, the other engines were bustling around. Everyone was working hard to prepare for the Ocean Life Exhibit, which was coming to the Island of Sodor. James and Cranky the Crane were busy unloading a big shipment of ocean plants. The plants would be put in the fish tanks to make the fish feel at home.

"Can I help?" asked Thomas.

"Oh, little Thomas. An engine like me doesn't need help," said James.

27
FRAGILE
GLASS
THIS END
UP
FISH TANKS
HANDLE WITH CARE
HARV

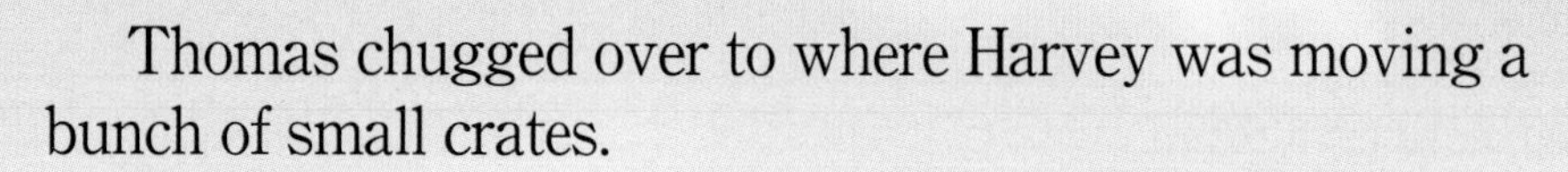

Thomas chugged over to where Harvey was moving a bunch of small crates.

"Keep back, little Thomas . . . these crates are full of all the empty fish tanks and they are very fragile," said Harvey. "We don't need you to be breaking anything."

As Thomas moved off, he noticed two cars coupled to Salty on the next track. He had never seen cars like this before. They were large and Thomas could see through their sides. They were full of water! A big octopus was swimming in the rear car. Thomas was amazed.

Then he pulled up to the front car. It had a huge shark in it. The shark looked at Thomas and opened his mouth. He had rows of big, scary teeth.

"Look at that!" Thomas gasped, and hurried up to find Salty.

"Amazin', aren't they, these critters from the deep? Eh, Thomas?" said Salty.

"Where are they from, Salty?" Thomas asked excitedly. "Where are they going?"

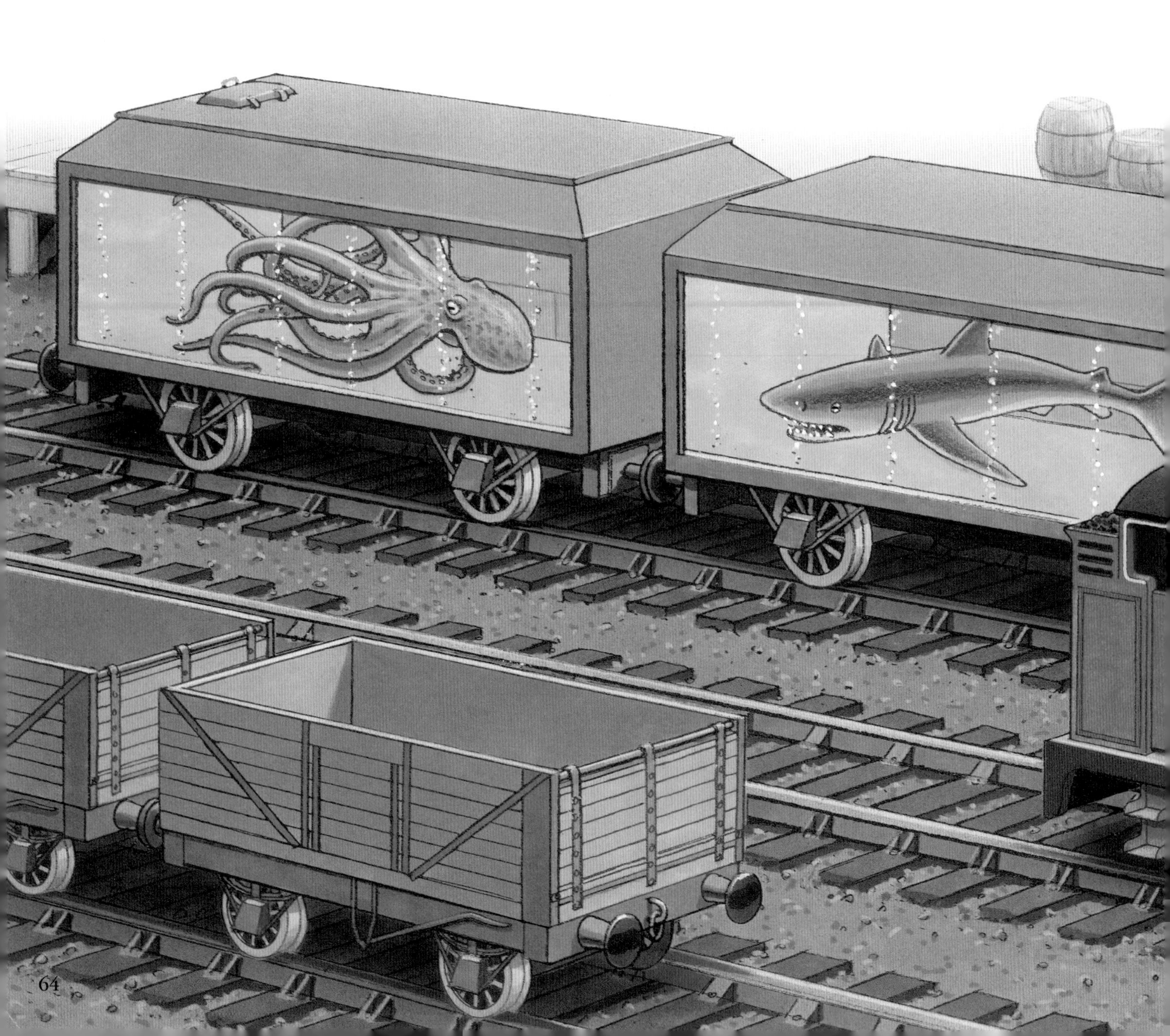

“They’re off to an ocean show in Tidmouth. It sure is fun havin’ ’em here, don’t you think?” answered Salty with a smile.

*I can’t wait to tell Percy about them,* thought Thomas. *Maybe we can see them in Tidmouth.*

Thomas was still marveling over the shark when Henry rushed by.

"Out of the way. I am in a hurry," Henry whistled.

"Don't fret, Thomas," said Salty. "Little engines can be mighty handy at times."

"Thanks, Salty," peeped Thomas sadly. "Maybe there's something I can do back at the station."

Just as Thomas was leaving the docks, Percy came chugging up, working hard, pulling the afternoon mail.

"Percy, you've got to take a look at the cars that Salty is—" Thomas started.

"Not now, Thomas," Percy interrupted. "I need to deliver this mail Right on Time." And he hurried past.

CRANKY
1

Percy passed Salty and then looked up and saw . . . a huge shark looking right at him!

"Yikes!" he tooted loudly, and rushed forward.

Percy was so surprised and so scared that he didn't look where he was going . . . Henry was stopped ahead of him on the same track. He was waiting for Harvey to cross with his fragile load.

Percy ran right into Henry, pushing him up the track . . . right toward Harvey's cargo of fish tanks.

"Watch out, Harvey!" tooted Henry.

Harvey looked back, saw Henry rushing at him, and went full steam ahead.

TOO LATE!

**CRASH!**

Henry crashed into Harvey's freight car!!

BULSTRODE
27
5
HARVEY

Harvey's freight car tipped off the track and the coupling snapped. Harvey, still at full steam, rushed forward.

He ran right into James. James was pushed off the track, which startled Cranky. Cranky let go of the crate he was carrying. The crate fell right onto James and burst, covering him with seaweed.

Thomas saw what happened and came hurrying back to help. His smaller size made it easy for him to fit between all the bumped engines and broken crates.

First, he helped pull Percy back on the track.

Then he kept the freight cars in order while the spilled mail and all the broken crates were cleaned up.

Finally, he helped Harvey put James back onto the track, and he didn't even tease James about his green face.

Later, when everything was in order again, he went to look at the shark, whose car was sitting on a siding.

Salty pulled up beside him. "Well, Thomas, I knew you'd find some way to prove what a Really Useful Engine you are," he said.

Thomas smiled and looked back at the shark, who gave him a big wink!

# THOMAS AND THE NAUGHTY DIESEL

Based on The Railway Series by The Reverend W Awdry
Illustrated by Richard Courtney and Josie Yee

Percy wasn't feeling well. Sir Topham Hatt sent him to the train doctor to get better.

"I shall have to borrow another engine while Percy is away," Sir Topham Hatt said.

The only engine the other railway could spare was Diesel.

Thomas the Tank Engine remembered how Diesel had caused trouble the last time he came to the station.

"You've come to help," Thomas said. "So no tricks."

"Tricks?" purred Diesel. "I'm just happy to help you Really Useful Engines again."

"Good," Thomas said. But he didn't believe Diesel.

Diesel set out to work. He was pulling freight cars when he met Toby.

"Oh!" Toby said. "It's you!" Toby remembered Diesel's mean tricks, too.

“After you finish your job here, please pull those freight cars to the harbor,” said Toby. He wanted Diesel as far from him as possible.

Thomas and Toby made it clear to Diesel that they would not stand for any nonsense.

"No making up stories or causing trouble," Thomas said.

"Yes, Thomas," Diesel purred. "I understand, Thomas."

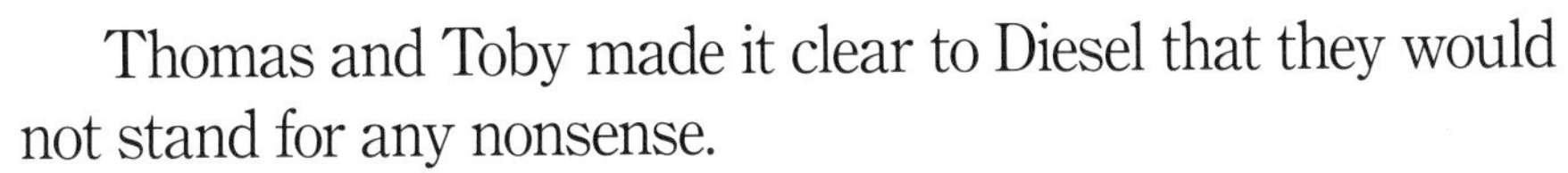

The freight cars knew the Sir Topham Hatt had sent Diesel away for trouble-making in the past.

"Let's have some fun with him," laughed the freight cars.

"There's Naughty Diesel," they called.

Diesel could feel his temper rising.

"Yes, Thomas," teased the freight cars. "I understand, Thomas."

"Grrrrrr!" Diesel roared. "I'll teach you!"

He gave the freight cars a great big push.

*Crash!*
Diesel pushed the freight cars right into a fence!
Broken wood and upset freight cars were everywhere!

“Grrrrrr!” Diesel growled. “Any more teasing, and I’ll squash you *all* flat!”

Sir Topham Hatt was very angry at Diesel.

"You're going back to the railway as soon as you're finished with your work!" said Sir Topham Hatt.

Diesel was sad that Sir Topham Hatt was angry with him.

1

Later that day, Daisy was chugging along when she realized she had an oil leak.

"Thomas will have to take your passengers," said her driver.

Thomas started up the hill, but the tracks were oily and he began to slip.

"Help! Help!" said Thomas.

Thomas could not stop his heavy train from pulling him downhill. Suddenly, Clarabel's back wheels rolled off the track and into the mud!

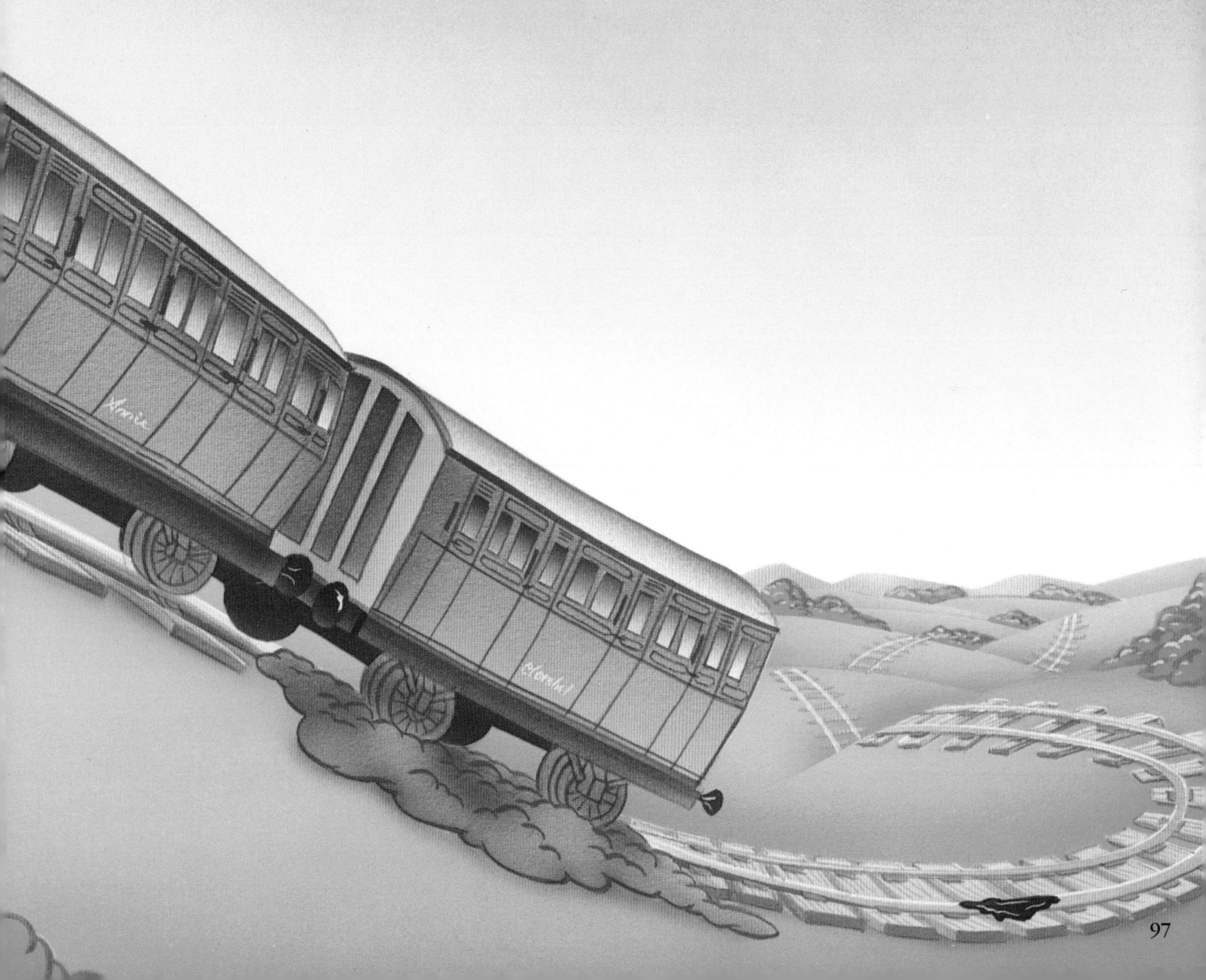

1

"Serves him right," Diesel said when he heard about Thomas.

But then Diesel felt ashamed. Thomas needed help! And Diesel was the closest and strongest engine on the line.

"I'm coming, Thomas!" Diesel called.

Bit by bit, Diesel crept forward on the oily track until he reached Thomas.

Soon workmen arrived and helped Clarabel back on the line. They cleaned the oil off the tracks and put dry sand on them.

Diesel dug his wheels into the sand and pushed Clarabel. Thomas helped, too.

Inch by inch, the engines moved forward. Finally, they chugged back to the station.

"Thank you, Diesel," said Clarabel.

"You were great!" Thomas said.

And even Sir Topham Hatt was proud of Diesel because he had rescued Thomas and Clarabel. Everyone hoped Diesel would come again.

Diesel hoped so, too.

# The Monster under the Shed

Based on The Railway Series by The Reverend W Awdry

Illustrated by Richard Courtney

It was a dark, blustery evening at the station. Sir Topham Hatt had closed the railway early on account of the weather. The engines were waiting for the signal to return to their sheds.

"Maybe one of us should tell a story to pass the time," Thomas suggested.
The other engines looked pleased with Thomas' idea.
"I have the perfect story for tonight," James volunteered with a sly grin.

“A long time ago,” James began, “there was a brave blue engine who was always eager to help.

“‘Blue engine,’ the stationmaster asked one night, ‘would you go to the end of the tracks to pick up a coach that was left behind?’

“‘Of course,’ the brave, eager engine replied. And he set out into the dark, foggy night.

“But by the time the little blue engine reached the end of the tracks, the fog was so thick he could hardly see anything.

“‘I’ll just have to wait until morning,’ said the engine to himself. And he settled into an old shed for the night.

"Late that night, the little blue engine awoke to a noise coming from below the shed.

"*Crreeeak*!

"He opened his eyes and saw long fingers reaching for him through the floorboards. There was a monster under the shed! Terrified, the little blue engine raced out of the shed with the horrible engine-eating monster chasing him through the fog."

"Th-then what happened?" Percy asked timidly.

"That's where the story ends," said James. "No one ever heard from that little blue engine again."

"What about the monster?" Percy whispered.

"Don't be silly, Percy," Gordon said with a chuckle. "It's just a story."

"What if that story is true?" Percy asked Thomas on their way to the sheds. "What if the engine-eating monster is out there somewhere right now?"

"Stop being such a scaredy-cat, Percy," Thomas answered. "There are no such things as monsters."

Later that night, after they had settled in for bed, the engines were startled by a terrible racket coming from Percy's Shed.

"Gordon, Thomas, help! There's a monster in my Shed!" wailed Percy.

Suddenly, James appeared, roaring with laughter. He had been rattling some scrap metal behind the sheds to frighten Percy.

"I'm a monster! I'm a monster!" James shouted.

Percy was embarrassed for making such a fuss.

"It's okay, Percy," said Henry. "Sometimes good imaginations think bad thoughts."

Later that night, Thomas woke with a fright. He heard a strange noise.

*Scratch, scratch.*

"Stop it, James!" Thomas yelled.

But James was sound asleep.

*Scratch, scratch.*

"If it's not James, then maybe I really do have a monster under my Shed," thought Thomas. And he stayed awake all night just to be safe.

Thomas was awfully tired when he met Percy at the docks the next morning.

"Did you hear any other strange noises in your Shed last night?" Thomas asked.

"Not after James' silly prank," Percy replied.

Now Thomas felt silly himself for staying awake all night.

By the middle of the day, Thomas was very sleepy and running far behind schedule. Henry pulled up beside him.

"You look as if you could use some special coal," said Henry.

"Oh, I'm just a little tired," Thomas answered. He didn't want anyone to know that he'd been too frightened to sleep.

Just then, James sped by on the express track.
"What's the matter, Thomas?" he called. "Monsters keeping you up at night?"
And James disappeared down the track, laughing loudly.

By the end of the day, Thomas barely had enough steam to make it back to the yard. The other engines were telling stories again, but Thomas headed straight to bed.

Sometime that night, Thomas woke with a fright.
*Scratch, scratch.*
The noises were back, and they were definitely coming from under the Shed.
"Who's there?" Thomas whispered into the dark.
*Crreeeak, crreeeak* came the answer.
"Go away, monster. Get out!" Thomas ordered as he closed his eyes tight.

*Thump, thump!*
*Thump, thump!*

The noise was getting louder—and *closer*!

"That will surely wake the other engines," Thomas said to himself. "They'll save me from the monster."

But the other engines didn't stir.

*Thump, thump.*

"It's just outside the door," Thomas yelped. "There's its head!"

"Help, Gordon," Thomas whispered.

But only the monster heard him.

*Thump, thump! Thump, thump!*

Then the doors of Thomas' Shed began to rattle on their hinges.
*BANG, BANG, BANG, BANG!*
"It's trying to get in!" thought Thomas.
Then, suddenly, the banging stopped.

Thomas was too frightened to move. He peered out into the dark. And there it was—the horrible engine-eating monster! Thomas could see its eyes glowing in the night.

Thomas clamped his own eyes shut and screamed.

"Gordon, Henry, Percy, James," he cried. "Save me from THE MONSTER!"

"Thomas," Gordon said, laughing, "open your eyes."

"What are you laughing at, Gordon?" snapped Thomas. "There's a monster right outside my Shed!"

# LOST AT SEA!

Based on The Railway Series by The Reverend W Awdry
Illustrated by Tommy Stubbs

It was a beautiful day on the Island of Sodor, and Thomas was very busy. A new Search and Rescue Center was being built, and there was a lot of work to do.

The Rescue Center would be a place to help people in trouble—plus Harold would have a new landing pad,

Captain would get a dock,

and Rocky would finally get his own Shed.

"The Search and Rescue Center will be made of the strongest wood of all—jobi wood," said Sir Topham Hatt. "It will arrive today at Brendam Docks."

Diesel wanted to show off and move all the jobi wood by himself. But when he did, the flatbeds holding the wood skipped off the track and over a steep cliff. Thomas saved Diesel, but all the wood splashed into the ocean below.

As a reward, Thomas was given the job of going to the Mainland to get more jobi wood. But the next day, the Dock Manager told him there was no room on the steamboat. Then Thomas saw a raft.

"The ship could pull me on that," Thomas puffed.

The engines whistled and *wheeshed* farewell to Thomas. He peeped goodbye to them. Then, with a long, low hoot of its horn, the big steamboat set out to sea, pulling Thomas on the raft.

Thomas was far out at sea when darkness started to fall. Suddenly he heard a creak and felt the raft lurch.

"Fizzling fireboxes!" he peeped. "The chain to the steamboat has snapped!"

Nobody heard Thomas whistle and peep for help as the steamboat chugged away. Waves rocked the raft. Mist gathered around him. Thomas was alone and very, very worried.

"How will I get home?" Thomas wondered.

The next morning, Thomas found himself on a strange island. It was misty and quiet and he didn't see any other engines.

"There must be a big dock and some ships," he said to himself. "If I find them, I can sail back to Sodor."

Thomas searched all over the island. He found many twisty tracks and thick, scratchy bushes. There was even a tunnel through an old fallen tree. But he didn't find a dock or anyone who could help him.

Meanwhile, on Sodor, Sir Topham Hatt learned that Thomas was missing. Everyone stopped working on the Search and Rescue Center and started looking for their lost friend. Sir Topham Hatt and Captain raced out to sea.

The engines searched all over Sodor, and Harold took to the sky.

Thomas was beginning to worry that he wouldn't find anyone to help him when he met three engines named Bash, Dash, and Ferdinand. They worked in an old logging camp.

"We're the Logging Locos," puffed Dash.

"You're on Misty Island," huffed Bash.

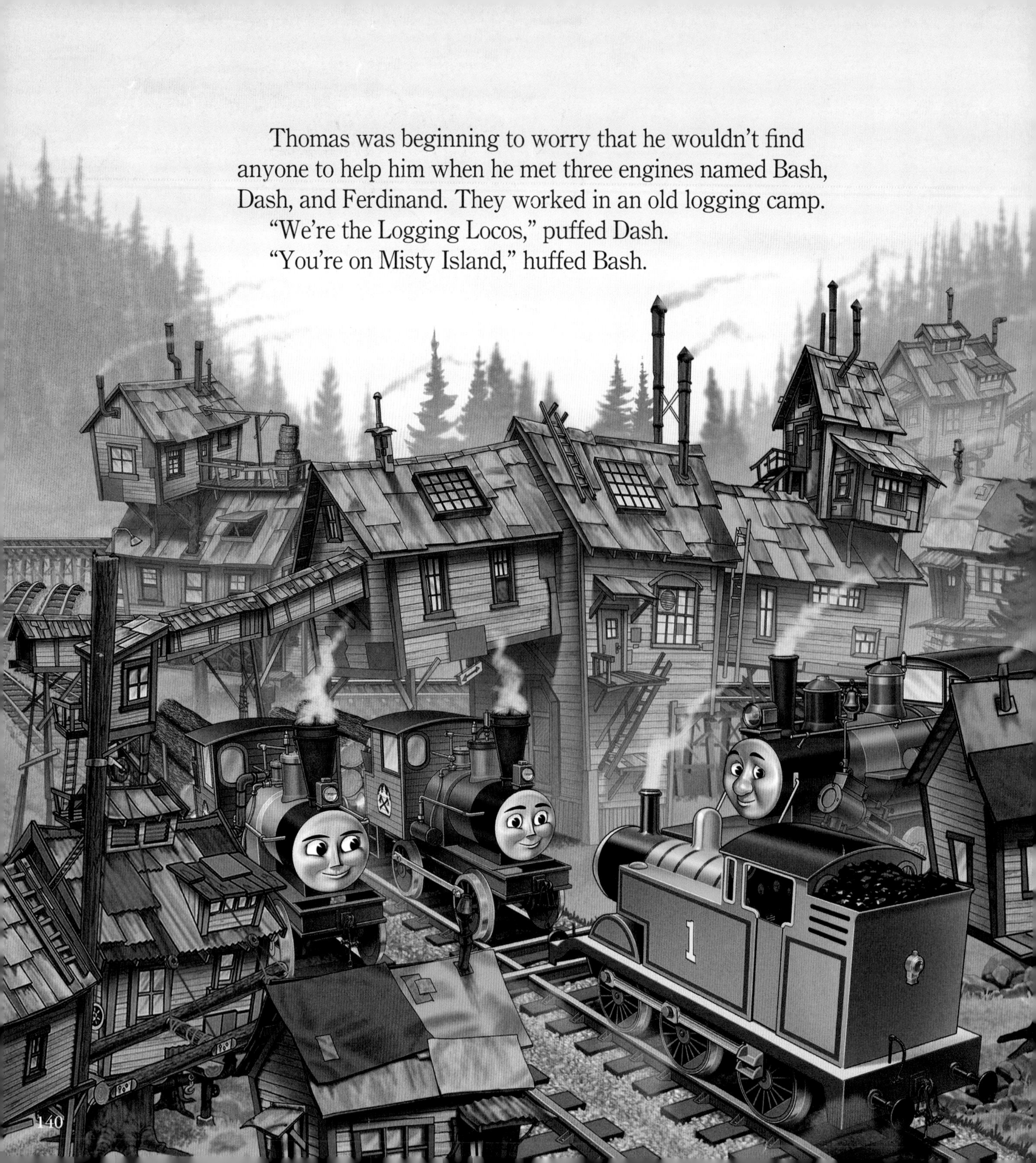

Then Thomas made an incredible discovery. "Bumpers and buffers! These are jobi logs. That's the wood we need to build the Sodor Search and Rescue Center."

Thomas told the Logging Locos about the Rescue Center. They agreed to help him load the wood.

But Bash, Dash, and Ferdinand liked playing games more than they liked loading logs—and they really loved bouncing on the wibbly, wobbly Shake Shake Bridge.

Thomas definitely did not enjoy bouncing on the bridge.

Ol' Wheezy, the giant log loader, wasn't much help, either. He wanted to throw wood instead of stacking it. Thomas thought the work would never get done, but after a day of biffing and bashing, the jobi wood was ready to go.

"Now how will I get these logs back to Sodor?" Thomas peeped.

Luckily, Bash knew a way.

Bash told Thomas about a dangerous old tunnel that connected Misty Island to Sodor.

"I know all about tunnels," Thomas puffed. "It won't be dangerous."

So, pushing their flatbeds, the Logging Locos followed Thomas into the dark and twisty tunnel.

Suddenly there was trouble.

*Boom! Crash!* Rocks tumbled down around the engines. The tracks were blocked. Thomas and the Logging Locos were trapped!

"I feel air on my funnel," Ferdinand peeped.

Dash spotted a hole in the roof of the tunnel.

"Huff your hardest," he said to Thomas. "Someone will see your steam."

Thomas thought that was an excellent idea and excitedly started puffing.

Back at Brendam Docks, Percy saw three puffs of steam in the sky. His firebox fizzed.

"It's Thomas!" Percy peeped to Whiff. "He's on Misty Island."

Whiff knew about an old tunnel that led to Misty Island. "Follow me," he puffed.

Percy and Whiff raced through the tunnel and found the cave-in.

"Watch out, Thomas," Whiff huffed. "Percy and I are going to push through the rocks."

With that, Percy and Whiff rocked and rolled and pumped their pistons. Then they crashed through the rocks. Thomas and the Logging Locos were saved!

Sir Topham Hatt was very happy that Thomas and his new friends were safe—and with all that new jobi wood, the Rescue Center would be finished in no time.

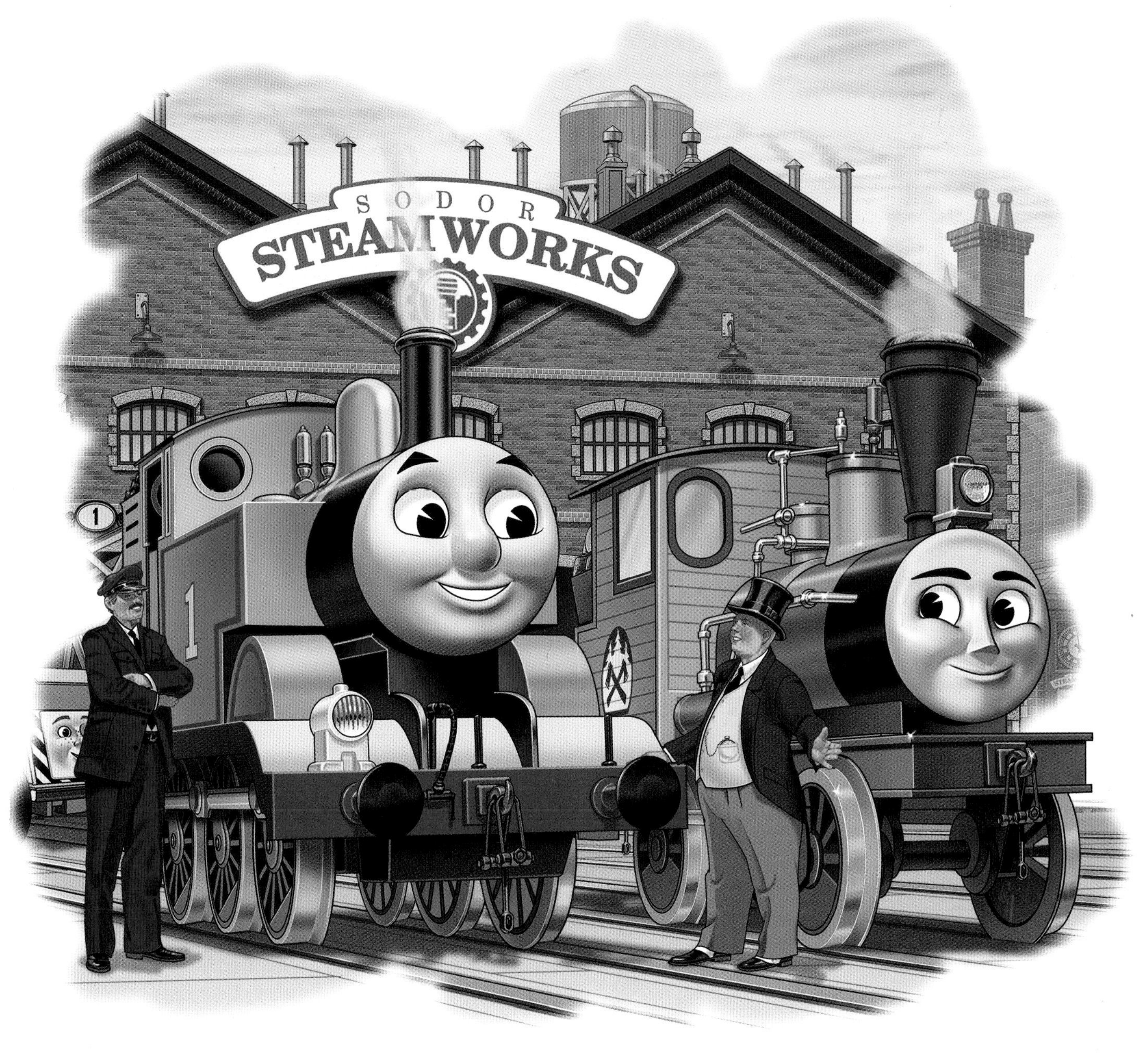

“Today is a special day made possible by very special engines,” Sir Topham Hatt announced at the opening of the Search and Rescue Center.

All the engines peeped, and Thomas’ pistons pumped with pride.

# Thomas Gets a Snowplow

Based on The Railway Series by The Reverend W Awdry
Illustrated by Richard Courtney

Early one winter morning, Thomas rolled out of his Shed to check the weather. It had snowed a little each day all week. It wasn't snowing just then, but the sky was gray and threatening.

"Looks like we're going to have to get out your snowplow soon, Thomas," said his driver.

Thomas was a Really Useful Engine, but he did not like wearing a snowplow. "No!" he said with a frown. "I'm fine just as I am. Besides, my branch line was clear yesterday. I don't *need* a snowplow. It's not even snowing!"

"But, Thomas," said his driver, "your snowplow would help you be Really Useful. Why don't you want to use it?"

"Snowplows look silly!" Thomas grumbled. "The other engines will laugh at me."

His driver looked up at the cloudy sky and back down at Thomas. "Well, it isn't snowing yet," he said. "Maybe you won't need your snowplow today after all. But you haven't used it since last winter, and we need to make sure it's still in working order. So you're going to have to try it on."

“All right,” Thomas grumbled reluctantly.

When he saw the snowplow, Thomas felt like steaming away. He *really* didn’t want to put it on, but he had agreed. So with a few turns of a screw and a few twists of a bolt, Thomas had a snowplow attached to his front.

“There now!” said his driver. “It fits perfectly.”

Just then, James and Henry pulled out of the Shed and saw Thomas.

"Ha! Look, Henry," said James. "Thomas is wearing a snowplow! It looks like a tin can!"

The two engines chuckled and chortled. "It's not even snowing! *I* wouldn't need a snowplow in this weather," Henry said. "I'm big enough to get through plenty of snow without one!"

Thomas blushed and looked down. "Please take it off," he whispered to his driver.

"All right," said his driver kindly. "But we may need to come back for it," he added, with another nervous glance at the sky.

When Thomas started out, there was some snow on the ground, but the tracks were clear. He didn't need a snowplow at all!

His first stop was at a small station by an inn. As Thomas was pulling up, it started snowing lightly. The innkeeper hurried out to unload supplies. "Mighty cold winter we're having, Thomas!" he said. "I'll need these extra blankets for my guests."

*"Peep, peep!"* And Thomas was off again.

Thomas' next stop was at the general store, where he had a large delivery to make. "Thank you, Thomas," said the owner of the store. "With this weather, I can *never* have enough snow shovels, hats, and mittens! My customers will be very happy."

Thomas smiled, peeped a farewell, and was on his way once more.

By the time Thomas made his last stop, it was snowing hard. The trip home was very difficult. The snow was piling up on the tracks, and it was hard to see. Thomas just went steadily on, concentrating on his warm Shed and the other engines waiting for him at the end of the line.

*See,* Thomas thought, *I can do this* without *a silly snowplow.*

Finally, Thomas managed to get back to the sheds. Percy, James, and Henry were talking about the snow. "I've never seen it snow so hard," said Percy.

Suddenly Sir Topham Hatt hurried in. "Toby is stuck on his branch line!" he said. "We need to go get him or he may be out in the snow all night. Henry, you're the biggest engine here, so you will have to do it."

"But it's snowing so hard, and it is so cold," said Henry.

Sir Topham Hatt gave Henry a stern look.

Henry quickly changed his mind and said, "But I am faster than Percy, James, or Thomas, *and* I'm big enough to get through this snow without a snowplow." So Sir Topham Hatt climbed aboard, and they were off.

Thomas' driver looked with concern at the swirling snowstorm. "I'm putting on your snowplow," he said. "I have a bad feeling about this snow."

So with a few turns of a screw and a few twists of a bolt, Thomas had his snowplow on again.

Just then, the engines saw a strange sight. It was hard to tell in the thick snow, but it looked like Henry, backing up into the yard.

"I couldn't make it," Henry steamed as he came closer. "The track was covered in snow. I almost got stuck. I could barely back out."

Thomas thought about how the other engines had laughed at his snowplow. Then he thought about Toby having to stay out in the snow all night. "Sir, with my snowplow, I can do it!" Thomas said.

The snow was deep along the track, but that was no problem for Thomas' snowplow. It was still hard to see, but Thomas went slowly and carefully.

Soon Thomas could tell that what looked like a mound of snow on the track ahead of him was actually Toby, buried deep.

"*Peep, peep!* Toby! I'm here to help you!" called Thomas.

Thomas crept past Toby and switched onto the same track. He carefully backed up to Toby. His driver jumped down and hooked them together. "Now pull!" his driver called.

Thomas pulled. He pulled as hard as he could. Slowly but surely, Toby began to move. And slowly but surely, Thomas pulled Toby through the snowstorm.

"Thank you, Thomas," said Toby. "I would've been out in the cold all night if it weren't for you and your snowplow. I wish a snowplow would fit over *my* cowcatcher!"

Sir Topham Hatt smiled and said, "Yes, Thomas, you are a Really Useful Engine, and today you are a hero as well."

Thomas beamed. For once he was happy to be wearing his snowplow . . . no one could see him blushing.

# DANGER AT THE DIESELWORKS

Based on The Railway Series by The Reverend W Awdry
Illustrated by Tommy Stubbs

The sky over the Island of Sodor was usually calm and blue. But one day, as Thomas and Percy were enjoying a ride in the countryside, they saw black clouds of smoke. They knew there was a fire, and they raced to help.

An old farm shed was in flames. Thomas and Percy let the farmhands take buckets of water from their tanks. Luckily, a new engine named Belle arrived. She could shoot water from her tanks. The flames fizzled and went out.

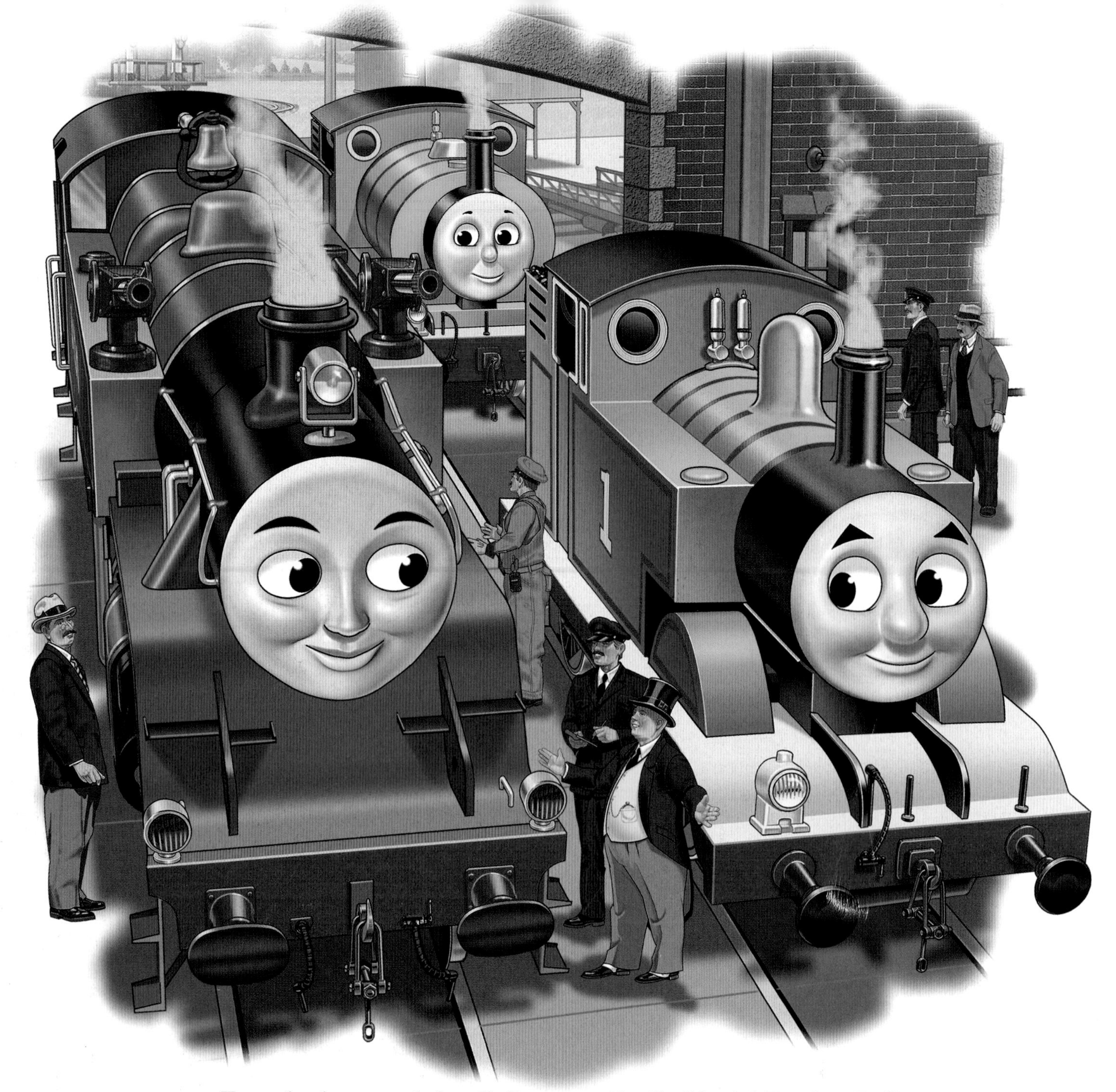


Everybody agreed that Belle was a Really Useful Engine. Belle was happy to help, but she knew Sodor needed a real fire engine.

"You need Flynn the Fire Engine. He's a real hero!" she peeped.

Sir Topham Hatt thought this was an excellent idea.

The next day, Thomas took Belle on a
of the Island of Sodor. They visited Brend
Docks, Knapford Station, and Thomas' Br
Line. Belle liked everything she saw.

Thomas and Belle didn't ask Percy to go with them on the tour. Diesel noticed that Percy was lonely and slid up next to him.

"Thomas is very busy with that new blue engine," Diesel hissed. He invited Percy to visit the Dieselworks.

Percy wasn't sure he should go to the Dieselworks. Thomas always said Steamies shouldn't puff there—but Thomas didn't seem to care about Percy lately.

Percy slowly rolled to the Dieselworks. His axles tingled.

"Hello, Percy!" boomed Diesel 10. "What an honor. Please come in."

The Dieselworks was dark, grimy, and a little scary, but the engines were all very nice, especially Den and Dart. They fixed the Diesels, but they didn't even have a crane!

"You should tell Sir Topham Hatt you need a new Dieselworks," puffed Percy.

"He doesn't listen to Diesels," said Diesel 10.

Percy had an idea. "I'll ask Thomas to tell Sir Topham Hatt. He always listens to Thomas."

Diesel 10 smiled.

When Percy returned to the Steamworks, he saw that Flynn the Fire Engine had arrived. Everyone was impressed by Flynn because he was bold and red and shiny. Percy felt very unimportant indeed.

Only Kevin listened to Percy's story. Kevin couldn't believe the Dieselworks didn't have a crane.

"Kevin, if you were there, you'd be a hero," Percy puffed.

Kevin liked the idea of being a hero very much.

That night, when Percy returned to Tidmouth Sheds, he saw something that made his boiler bubble—Flynn was in *his* berth!

"If I'm not wanted here," Percy thought, "I'll go someplace where they do like me."

Percy found Kevin, and together they rolled to the Dieselworks. They stayed there all night—something no Steamie had ever done before.

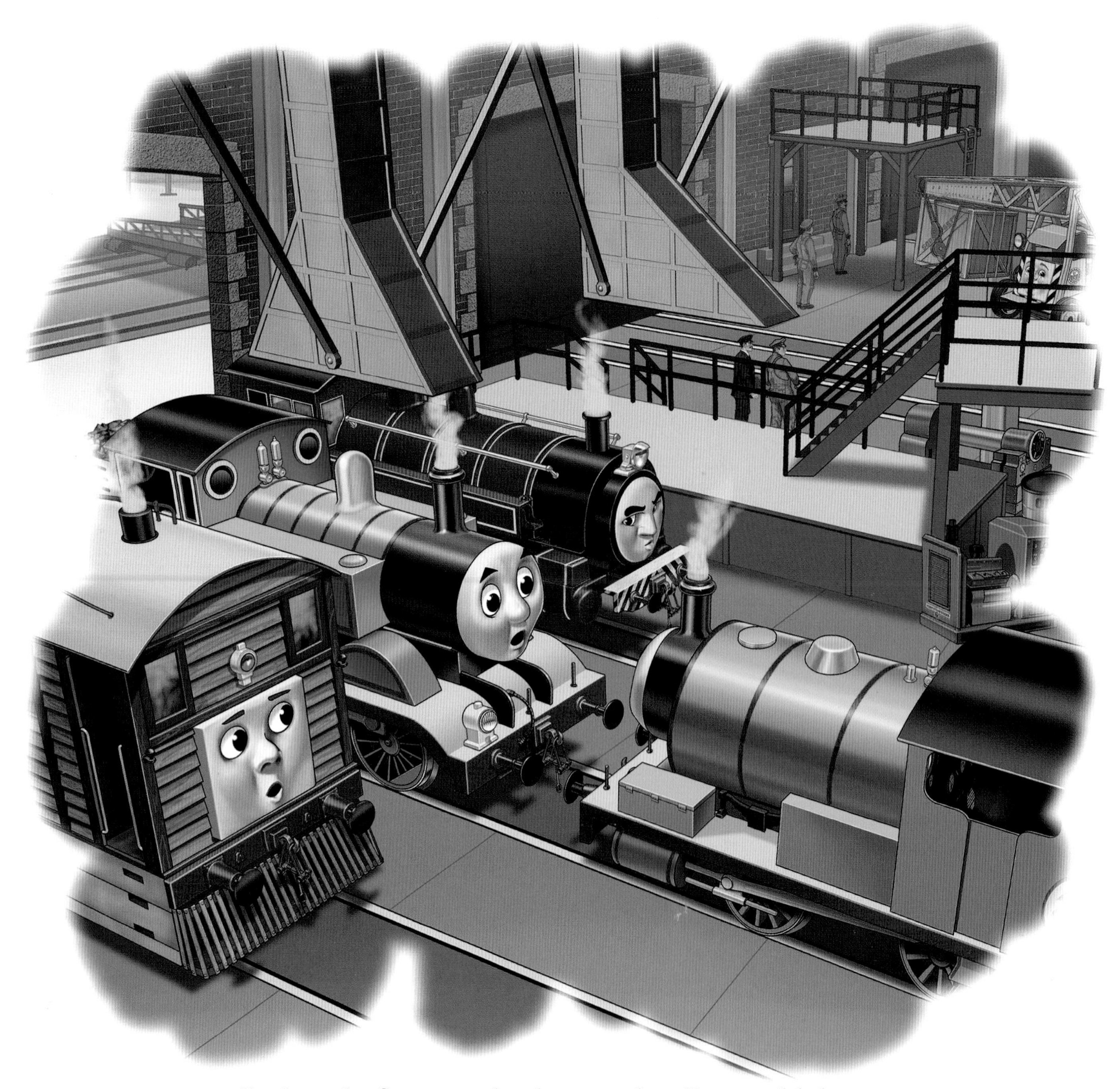

Back at the Steamworks the next day, Percy told the steam engines where he had been. Everyone was shocked. Thomas' firebox fizzled.

Victor was angry that Kevin was still at the Dieselworks. He rattled off to tell Sir Topham Hatt.

Percy and Thomas raced to the Dieselworks. Thomas said he would help them get a new building. But Diesel 10 wasn't interested.

"Since Victor isn't at the Steamworks, we're going to take it over—and we want you to lead us, Percy!"

Percy proudly led the Diesels to the Steamworks, but when they got there, no one listened to him.

"The Steamworks is ours," roared Diesel 10. "And we're not giving it back!"

Worst of all, Diesel 10 said Thomas was being held prisoner at the Dieselworks.

Percy knew he'd made a terrible mistake. He quickly went back to the Dieselworks, where Den and Dart were holding Thomas. As Percy screeched to a stop, sparks from his wheels started a fire! Now he had to save Thomas *and* put out a fire!

Percy knew that only one engine could help him now. He raced to find Flynn the Fire Engine. Percy found him at the Sodor Search and Rescue Center. With pistons pumping, the two engines puffed to save Thomas.

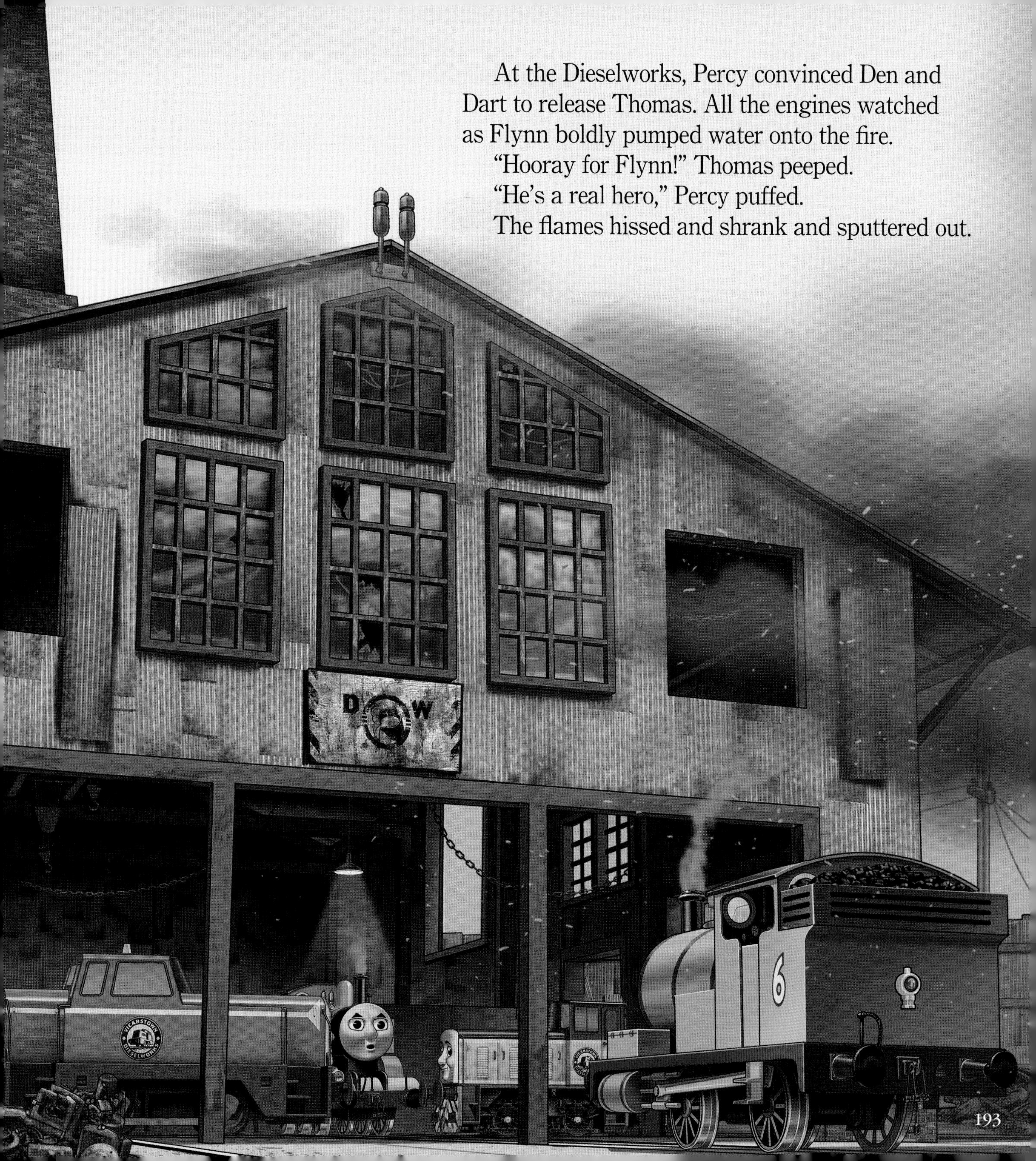


At the Dieselworks, Percy convinced Den and Dart to release Thomas. All the engines watched as Flynn boldly pumped water onto the fire.

"Hooray for Flynn!" Thomas peeped.

"He's a real hero," Percy puffed.

The flames hissed and shrank and sputtered out.

Thomas and Percy collected all the Steamies and hurried to save the Steamworks. The Diesels refused to leave.

"Taking things and using trickery is wrong," Thomas peeped. "We can help you get a new Dieselworks, but you have to be fair with us."

Suddenly, Sir Topham Hatt arrived. He was very cross.

"Diesel 10," he said sternly. "You have caused confusion and delay. Because of you, none of my engines has been Really Useful."

Diesel 10 whimpered and his claw crumpled.

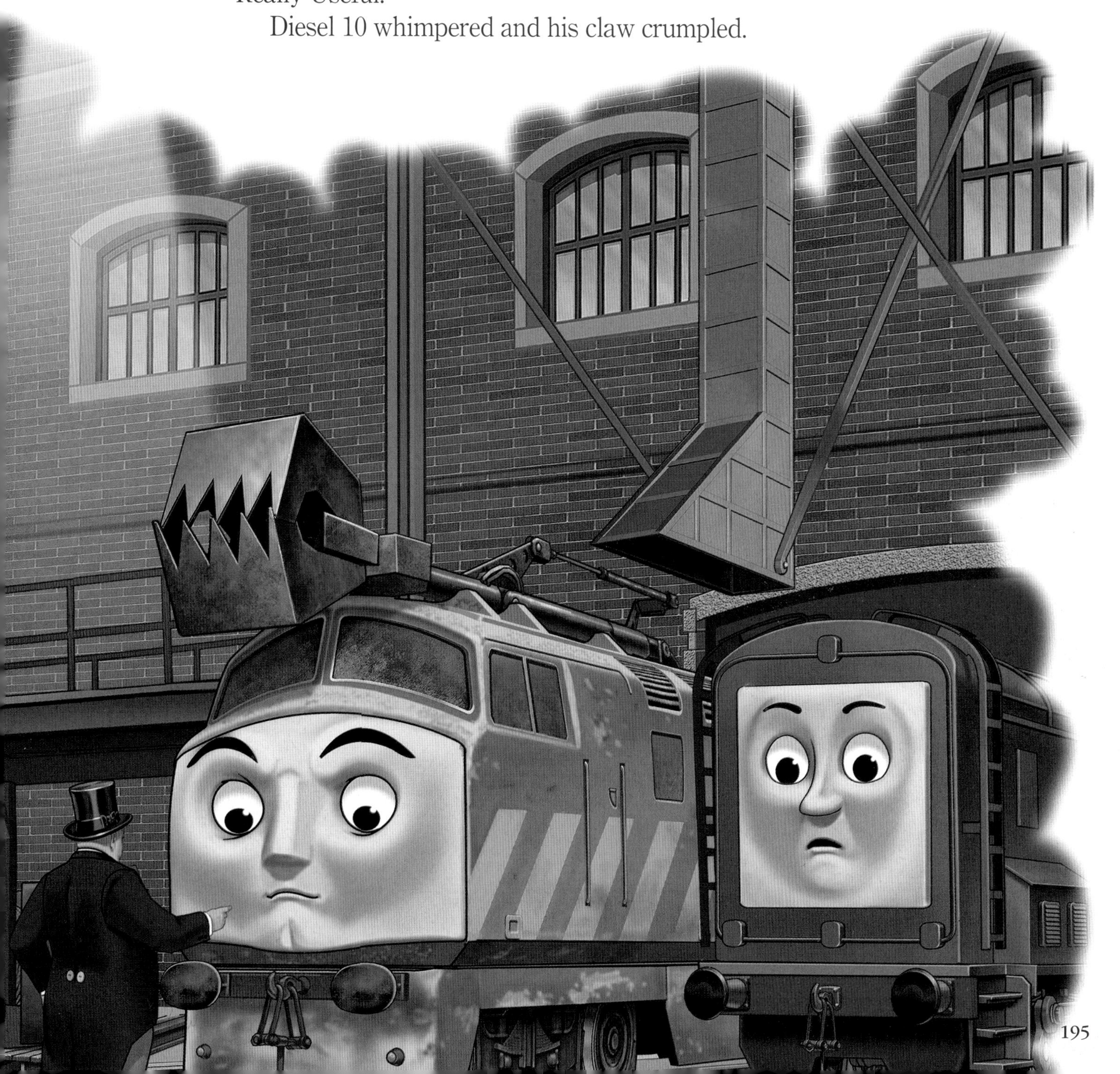

Sir Topham Hatt explained that the Diesels would get a new Dieselworks. “That was always my plan. Everything takes time. And everyone must wait their turn.”

The Diesels and the Steamies agreed to work together to build the new Dieselworks.

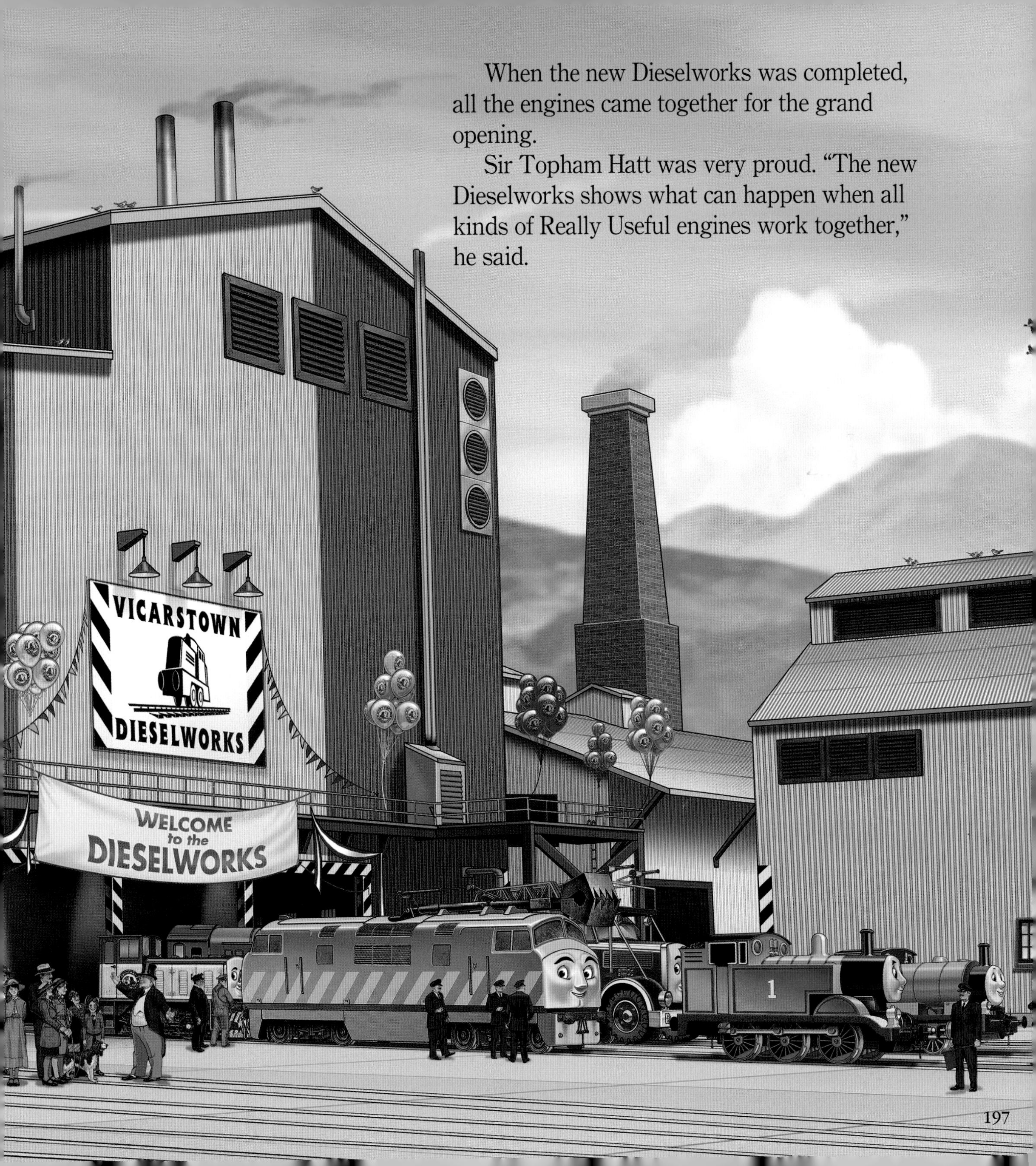


When the new Dieselworks was completed, all the engines came together for the grand opening.

Sir Topham Hatt was very proud. "The new Dieselworks shows what can happen when all kinds of Really Useful engines work together," he said.

Everyone cheered and all the engines peeped proudly. Percy and Thomas were especially happy. They were glad to be best friends again. They giggled and jiggled and puffed with joy.

# Calling All Engines!

Based on The Railway Series by The Reverend W Awdry
Illustrated by Richard Courtney

SODOR AIRPORT
Coming Soon!

Summer is a busy time on the Island of Sodor.

The engines love to show travelers around the island. They visit the seaside, the windmill, and the new Sodor Suspension Bridge.

One morning, Sir Topham Hatt came to the sheds. He had a very important announcement to make. “A new airport is to be built on Sodor and I need you all to help.”

The engines were very excited.

Thomas and Percy were coupled to freight cars full of bricks and timber to take to the airport building site.

"Imagine all the travelers," chuffed Thomas.

"And all the airplanes!" puffed Percy.

Then Arry and Bert arrived.

"Stinky steamies in the way again," mumbled Arry.

"Why do we have to work near them?" grumbled Bert.

This made Thomas and Percy cross. They didn't want to work near the diesels either. The diesels were oily, and they seemed very different to the steamies.

Thomas, Percy, Arry, and Bert worked at the airport all afternoon. They shunted freight cars full of bricks and tar.

The diesels bumped Thomas and biffed Percy.

"Dirty diesels," moaned Percy. "I don't like them!"

Thomas and Percy had been so excited about working at the airport, but Arry and Bert were there and now it wasn't any fun.

That night, a hurricane swept through the island. It was the strongest wind the engines had ever known. All night long, the wind howled down the tracks. It tore down the trees and ripped off roofs.

SODOR

The next morning, Thomas gasped at what he saw.

"Bust my buffers!" he cried. "Look at what the wind has done!"

The seaside had been battered, the windmill was wrecked, and the Sodor Suspension Bridge had collapsed. Thomas felt terrible.

Sir Topham Hatt came to see the engines. "The hurricane has done lots of damage," he said sadly. "Everyone will have to work even harder if we want to open the airport."

Edward and Henry brought bricks to the airport building site while Diesel arrived with a load of timber.

But the diesels weren't talking to the steam engines, and the steam engines weren't talking to the diesels.

Everyone was cross.

That afternoon, Thomas had to collect some paint for the bridge. He puffed into the builder's yard to pick up the pots of paint.

But Diesel was in the yard, too. "Now I'll show Thomas who's best," Diesel whispered. And he gave the freight cars an extra-hard shunt. Paint pots flew into the air and splattered down…

*. . . all over Thomas!*
Thomas looked very silly, indeed.
"Spotty boiler," laughed Diesel, and he rolled away.
"I'll show those diesels," Thomas huffed.

So the next time Thomas saw Arry, he gave him a biff.

And when Arry saw James, he gave him a bash.

Soon the diesels and the steamies were biffing and banging and being bashed all over the island.

The engines were in a terrible mess, and no work had been done.

That evening, Sir Topham Hatt came to see the engines. He was very angry. "You have caused confusion and delay. The seaside is still a mess. The bridge isn't painted. And we will not be able to open the airport. No travelers will come to Sodor this year!"

"No travelers," moaned Thomas.

"And no airplanes," groaned Percy.

All of the engines knew they had behaved badly, and they were very sad.

That night, Thomas had a dream. He was puffing along a misty mountain track. And there was Lady! Lady was a very special steam engine. She worked high up in the mountains.

Lady was shunting trucks with Rusty the diesel engine. Thomas was surprised.

"We always finish our jobs when we work together," puffed Lady.

The next morning when Thomas woke up, he had an idea.

First he went straight to see Mavis. Mavis was a kind diesel engine, and Thomas knew she would listen. He told Mavis that he wanted the steam engines and the diesels to work together.

Mavis agreed...it was the only way to get the airport open in time.

"Let's have a big meeting with all of the engines at the coaling stop tomorrow," Thomas puffed.

Thomas and Mavis went to see the other engines to tell them about the meeting.

Thomas told Percy…

then James…

then Emily.

Mavis told Diesel…

then Arry…

then Bert.

The next day, the engines gathered at the coaling stop. The steam engines and the diesels were all lined up. Thomas blew his whistle.

"Steamies and diesels need to work together," chuffed Thomas. "If the airport doesn't open, it will be bad for all the engines! Both steam engines and diesel engines need passengers and freight to be useful. If we work together, we can get the job done!" puffed Thomas.

All of the engines agreed.

MAVIS

After that, the engines worked harder than ever. They hauled bricks and timber and cleared away debris from the storm. They moved paint and tar and made sure there were enough workers to do each important job. And all the engines were careful not to bump or block each other. Even Diesel 10, the biggest diesel engine of all, agreed to help out! Soon the engines were even enjoying working together, smiling and joking as friends will do.

Before long, the airport was finished. It had shining buildings and a big tall control tower. And the runway was long and smooth. The engines were very proud. And very excited. . . .

"I can't *wait* for the travelers," puffed Thomas.

"And look!" peeped Percy. "Here comes thc first airplane."

# THOMAS AND THE MAGIC RAILROAD™

# DIESEL 10 Means Trouble

Based on The Railway Series by The Reverend W Awdry
Illustrated by Richard Courtney

Thomas the Tank Engine was a little blue engine who always tried to be Really Useful. He and all his friends lived on the Island of Sodor.

Life on the Island of Sodor was very peaceful and happy. But on this beautiful island where trains could talk and the railroad was really reliable and Right on Time, trouble was brewing. . . .

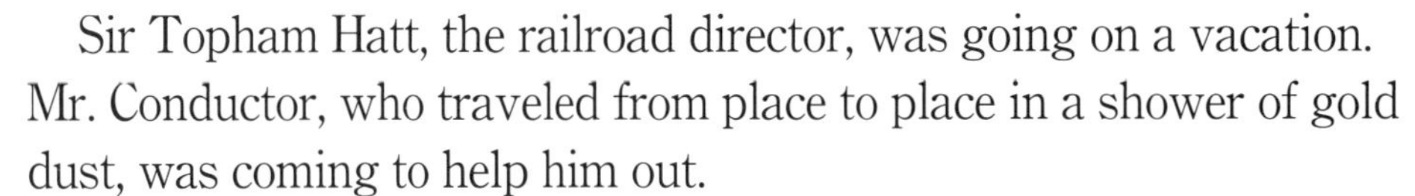

Sir Topham Hatt, the railroad director, was going on a vacation. Mr. Conductor, who traveled from place to place in a shower of gold dust, was coming to help him out.

"I have to go and meet Mr. Conductor," Thomas said. "He's going to take care of us while Sir Topham Hatt is away."

"I think we can take care of ourselves," huffed Gordon.

*Whoooosh!* Suddenly, a big diesel engine raced past them.
"Get out of my way, you blue puffballs!" the diesel growled.
"What was that?" asked Gordon nervously.

"*That* was a problem," Thomas said as the diesel screeched away. "That's Diesel 10. Sir Topham Hatt sent him to help us steam engines, but Diesel 10 is behaving as though he hates us. I think he's a really scary engine."

"Pah," grumbled Gordon. "Really Useful Engines like us have to be brave, little Thomas."

Thomas agreed, but he couldn't help feeling frightened.

Meanwhile, Diesel 10 was planning to get rid of the steam engines once and for all. *He* wanted to run the railroad.

That night, Diesel 10 sneaked up to the engine shed and threatened Mr. Conductor with his jagged claw. "Make the most of tonight, Twinkle-Toes," hissed Diesel 10. "Because you won't like tomorrow."

Mr. Conductor had another problem, too. “I’ve suddenly lost all my sparkle,” he sighed to Thomas. “To get it back, I must find some more gold dust.”

Thomas and the other engines knew they had to help Mr. Conductor find the source of the magic gold dust.

“While the boss, Sir Topham Hatt, is away, we cats will play,” purred Diesel 10 to his pals.

Splatter and Dodge gulped.

"We're going to make life miserable for those steaming heaps of trash on wheels," Diesel 10 continued. "This island doesn't need them. It needs diesels! There's no use for steam engines these days. They're history!"

"But what about Mr. Conductor?" asked Splatter.

"Isn't he going to stop us?" Dodge asked.

"Mr. Conductor needs his magic gold dust to keep an eye on us," snickered Diesel 10. "And I know he can't, because he's just run out."

A door opened on Diesel 10's cab roof, and out came his huge metal claw!

"I'll take care of all of them with this," said Diesel 10. He lifted his claw high above them—but then it dropped and hit him on the head!

"I don't think he meant to do that," Splatter and Dodge said to each other.

Little did the diesels know that Toby the Tram Engine had overheard their plans. Toby told the other engines. Then he followed the diesels to see what they were going to do next.

The diesels were plotting to destroy the magic buffers that led to Mr. Conductor's Magic Railroad.

"We don't know where the entrance to the Magic Railroad is, and we don't know which are the right buffers to destroy," said Diesel 10 to Splatter and Dodge. "So we'll have to destroy *all* of them."

Toby knew he had to do something to stop Diesel 10.
"I've got to distract him," thought Toby.
*Clang!* Toby rang his bell as loud as hc could.
"It's the old teapot!" shouted Diesel 10. "Smash him!"

Diesel 10 tried to catch Toby with his claw. But he knocked over a pile of scrap—right onto his own tracks! Diesel 10's path was blocked.

"Boss, did you mean to do that?" asked Splatter and Dodge.

"Grrrrr," Diesel 10 growled. "I always mean what I do."

Diesel 10 was mad when he found out that Thomas had traveled the Magic Railroad to bring back Lady the Golden Engine. Lady was the source of the magic gold dust. She could help Mr. Conductor foil Diesel 10's plans.

Diesel 10 chased Lady. But Thomas raced between them. All three engines headed toward a dangerous old viaduct.

Lady crossed the old viaduct. Stones began to fall. When Thomas crossed the viaduct, more stones fell and a big gap appeared in the track. Thomas jumped the gap just in time.

But Diesel 10 couldn't stop, and he tumbled far below onto a barge filled with sludge.

Lady was safe, and there would always be plenty of gold dust.

"You're a Really Useful Engine," Gordon told Thomas.

*"Peep! Peep!"* Thomas said, and puffed home into the sunset.

# Thomas-saurus Rex

Based on The Railway Series by The Reverend W Awdry
Illustrated by Richard Courtney

1

Thomas puffed into the Yard after a long day. He saw James and Gordon talking together. When he stopped at the water tower, he could hear everything they said.

1
4

"I am too important to pull such an ancient load," said Gordon.

"Yes," replied James. "I am glad they brought that old bucket of bolts to do it. The engines here are all too fine."

"I'm surprised he can do *anything,* he is so old."

"Well, it makes sense for him to pull that Special. The fossils deserve each other," said James. Both of the engines laughed.

Thomas wondered what they were talking about.

Percy was waiting when Thomas got to the shed.

"Did you see Stepney?" asked Percy. "Did you see what his Special is?"

"No, but I heard Gordon and James talking about it," answered Thomas. "They said it was a lot of old junk."

"I think it's kind of neat," said Percy.

"Don't let them hear you say that," said Thomas. "They'll tease you, too."

Thomas liked Stepney. Stepney was one of the oldest engines on the whole Island of Sodor. He had seen a lot and had interesting stories to tell.

Thomas' favorite story was about Sir Topham Hatt as a little boy.

One beautiful day, little Topham Hatt was out for a carriage ride with his grandfather. The horse was dashing through the countryside. Grandfather Hatt saw a rut in the road, but it was too late to swerve.

*CRACK!*

The carriage's axle was broken, and the horse ran off. Luckily, no one was hurt. But they were a long way from home.

Just then, Stepney, a brand-new engine, came chugging by. He was pulling a load of coal, so he didn't have any passenger coaches.

STEPNEY
55

There was only one thing to do. Topham Hatt and his grandfather crawled up on top of the pile of coal. And off they went.

When they got to town, little Topham Hatt was covered head to toe in coal dust. He was very dirty. And so was Grandfather, so Mother couldn't be cross. They both laughed—and even had their picture taken!

Thomas always liked that story, and Percy liked it, too. It made them laugh to think that Sir Topham Hatt was ever that dirty.

The next morning, Thomas went looking for Stepney.

"Good morning, sir," said Thomas politely.

"Well, hello, Thomas," said Stepney with a smile. "What do you think of my Special?"

Thomas looked at the rock with some bones in it and at the old chest. He didn't want to hurt Stepney's feelings. "It s-s-sure looks old," he stammered.

"It's the oldest thing I have ever pulled," laughed Stepney. "It makes me feel young. The chest is full of gems from Rolf's Castle in the days of knights."

"This fossil is from the age of dinosaurs. It is going to be part of the museum fair at Tidmouth. And so am I, because I am *so* old," he added proudly.

Thomas thought the things seemed pretty interesting, but he remembered Gordon and James saying they were junk. Thomas didn't know what to think.

Just then, Sir Topham Hatt came to see the engines. "Stepney and his Special must go to Tidmouth for the museum show," he said. "But the hill to Tidmouth may be too steep for Stepney with that valuable Special. So someone will need to help push from behind."

"Push? I would not *push* a Special made of solid gold," said Gordon, "let alone that pile of old junk. I only *pull* Specials, and important ones at that."

"I don't think we should have to push that Special, Sir," said James.

Thomas did not want the others to tease him. But he saw that Stepney looked sad that no one wanted to help him.

"I will push Stepney's Special," he quietly volunteered.

"Thank you, Thomas," said Sir Topham Hatt. "I appreciate it when engines prove that they are Really Useful." And then he gave Gordon a stern look.

Gordon puffed, and James gave a cheeky chuckle. "Better him than us," he said.

Thomas pushed the Special out of the Yard. He heard James call out, "Don't let them mistake you for that old junk and send *you* to the scrap yard."

All the way to Tidmouth, Thomas worried about what everyone would say about his old Special. He knew the children liked him, but would they think he was just an "old fossil" when he arrived with this "old junk"?

When they arrived at Tidmouth, there were already lots of interesting things to see. There was a butterfly tent, a petting zoo, and a frog exhibit. Thomas helped Stepney onto a special siding that allowed everyone to see the fossil and chest close up. But no one seemed to notice they were there.

And then Thomas heard one little boy shout with delight. “Look over there! It’s Thomas! And he brought a dinosaur!”

1
BUTTERFLY
PETTING ZOO

Soon Thomas and Stepney were surrounded.

"Cool!" "Wow!" "Look at that!"

Thomas had never heard the children so excited. He was excited, too.

Sir Topham Hatt walked over to them. Thomas was surprised to see that he looked dirty.

"Good work, Thomas!" said Sir Topham Hatt. "I should have come with you and Stepney. I got a flat tire. I haven't been this dirty in a long, long time." He laughed. "Do you remember that day on the coal car, Stepney?"

"I sure do," chuckled Stepney. "You were a happy little boy, Sir."

"Just like these children. They will never forget this day."

“And neither will I,” added Sir Topham Hatt.

Just then, a man with a camera walked up. He said, “Everyone smile and say ‘steamie!’”

*Flash!*

# The Lost Crown of Sodor

AS SEEN ON DVD!

KING OF THE RAILWAY — THE MOVIE

Based on The Railway Series by The Reverend W Awdry
Illustrated by Tommy Stubbs

CRANKY
Sodor Shipping Co
SODOR
SODOR
Sodor Shipping Co
Sodor Shipping Co

It was a busy day at Brendam Docks. Thomas and Percy were shunting trucks. One of the trucks bashed into Percy's buffer and tipped over. A crate fell out and split open.

"Look!" peeped Percy. "It's a metal man, a robot!"

"Silly," Cranky grumbled. "It's a suit of armor, like a knight used to wear."

"Cranky's right," said Sir Topham Hatt. "In the old days, the Island of Sodor was ruled by kings. The most beloved was King Godred. He lived in Ulfstead Castle and wore a golden crown. The crown disappeared long ago."

6

Sir Topham Hatt said that the ruins of Ulfstead Castle could be seen on the Earl of Sodor's estate.

The next morning, Thomas delivered a crate to the earl's estate. There he met Millie, the earl's Narrow Gauge engine.

"If only I had King Godred's golden crown," the earl said sadly.

Over the next few days, Thomas, James, and Percy made many deliveries to the earl's estate. Thomas saw his friend Jack the Digger there.

"I'm helping the earl restore Ulfstead Castle," Jack puffed.

"So *that's* his plan!" whistled Thomas.

When Thomas, Percy, and James were shunting containers, Thomas saw a flatbed holding a very large crate. The earl said it was a special delivery for the Steamworks. He climbed into Thomas' cab, and the three friends pulled the crate to the Steamworks.

When they got there, a gantry crane lifted the crate to reveal an old engine named Stephen. His wood was worn, and he had rust holes in his boiler. He hadn't run in years.

"Surprise!" the old engine peeped.

Victor said he'd have Stephen fixed up in no time.

The earl told Thomas he had a special job for Stephen. "But it's best not to say anything yet."

"I won't say a word," said Thomas. "I promise."

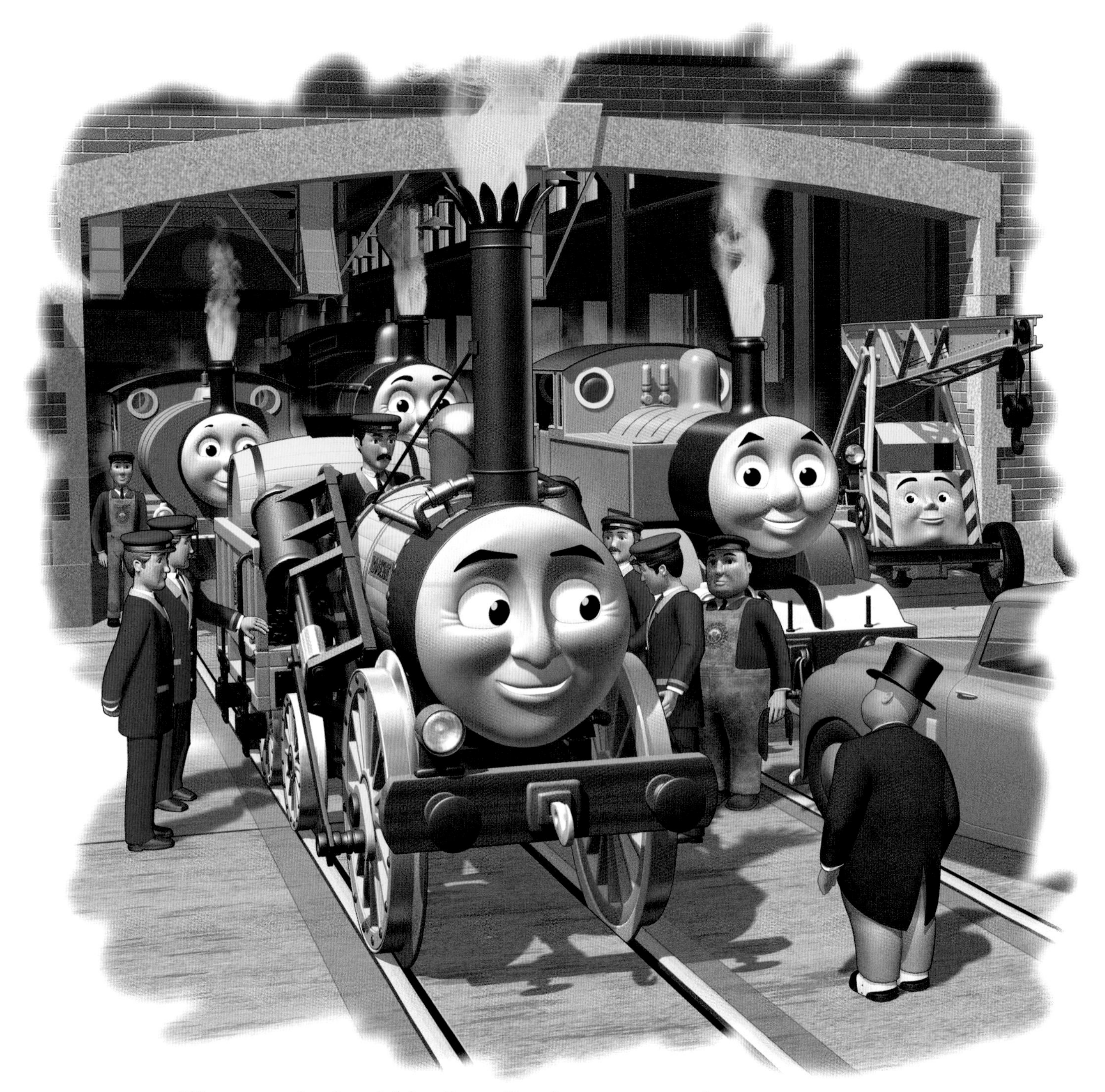

Victor worked quickly. Soon Stephen was good as new.

"You look Really Useful again," Thomas peeped.

Stephen had told the engines about his early days. "I worked so fast they called me the Rocket!" he said.

But what job would he do now?

As the others rolled away to work, Thomas saw that Stephen looked sad. So Thomas broke his promise and told Stephen that the earl had a special job for him.

Stephen was very excited.

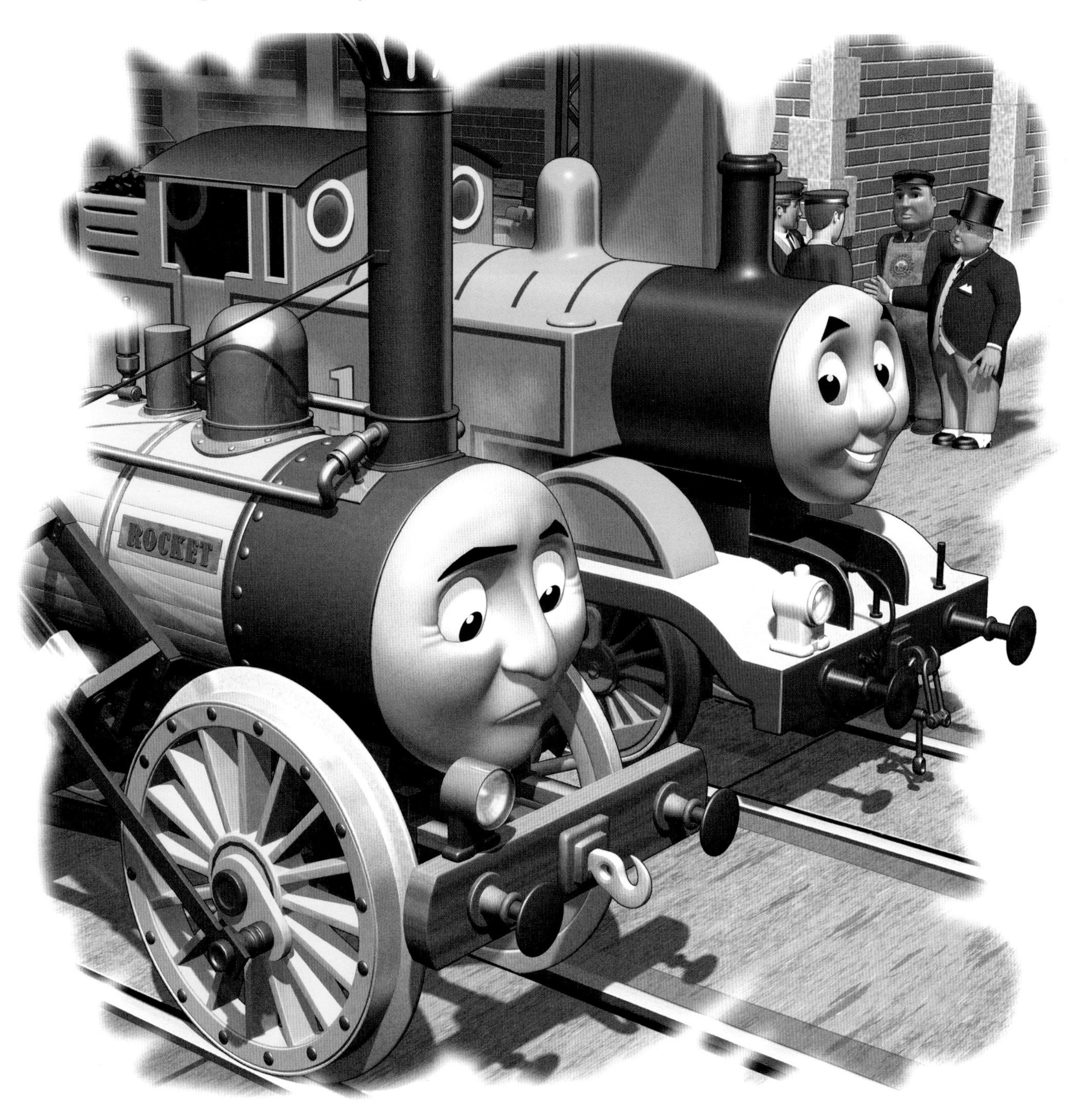

Thomas, James, and Percy steamed to the earl's estate.

Inside the castle walls, they were amazed to see a giant platform on rails. The earl called it the traveler.

"You three will move the traveler into place for the men. You must be careful to keep the platform stable."

Meanwhile, Stephen wanted to know about his special job, so he rolled off to Brendam Docks.

"There's no work here for an old engine like you," Cranky said.

Next, Stephen went to Blue Mountain Quarry.

"We can always use help," Luke peeped.

But the trucks Stephen tried to pull were too heavy. He steamed and strained, but they wouldn't move.

"When I worked in a mine, the trucks weren't this heavy," said Stephen. "Are there any mines around here?"

Skarloey told him there was an old mine near the castle ruins. "I don't think anyone works there now," he said.

Stephen found the entrance to the abandoned mine. He sighed.

"There's no job on this island for me!"

Nearby, Thomas was working with the Troublesome Trucks. Suddenly, the trucks slipped loose and roared down the hill, right toward Stephen! Stephen had no choice but to push into the mine. His funnel hit the roof and fell off. Rocks crashed down behind him, sealing up the entrance.

Stephen searched for a way out. He crept around dark bends and through empty tunnels, but the tracks just went in circles. The only thing he found was an old wooden crate.

Thomas and Percy searched for Stephen. At the entrance to the old mine, Thomas saw something familiar lying on the ground. It was Stephen's funnel!

Thomas chuffed away to get Jack the Digger. Jack cleared the mine entrance, and Thomas raced in.

"Stephen! Stephen!" he peeped.

Stephen heard Thomas, but he was too weak to move or even whistle.

Finally, Thomas turned a corner and saw a welcome sight.

Thomas pushed Stephen out of the mine. The earl was there to greet them.

"I found a big wooden chest in the mine," Stephen said.

"Wonderful!" the earl exclaimed. "But first we must get you ready for tomorrow. You are an engine with a special job to do!"

The next day, an excited crowd gathered around Ulfstead Castle.

"Welcome, ladies and gentlemen, engines and coaches," said the earl.

“Let me introduce my special steam engine, Stephen! He and Millie will be happy to show you the grounds.”

Stephen’s new funnel glittered like gold. It reminded Thomas of something.

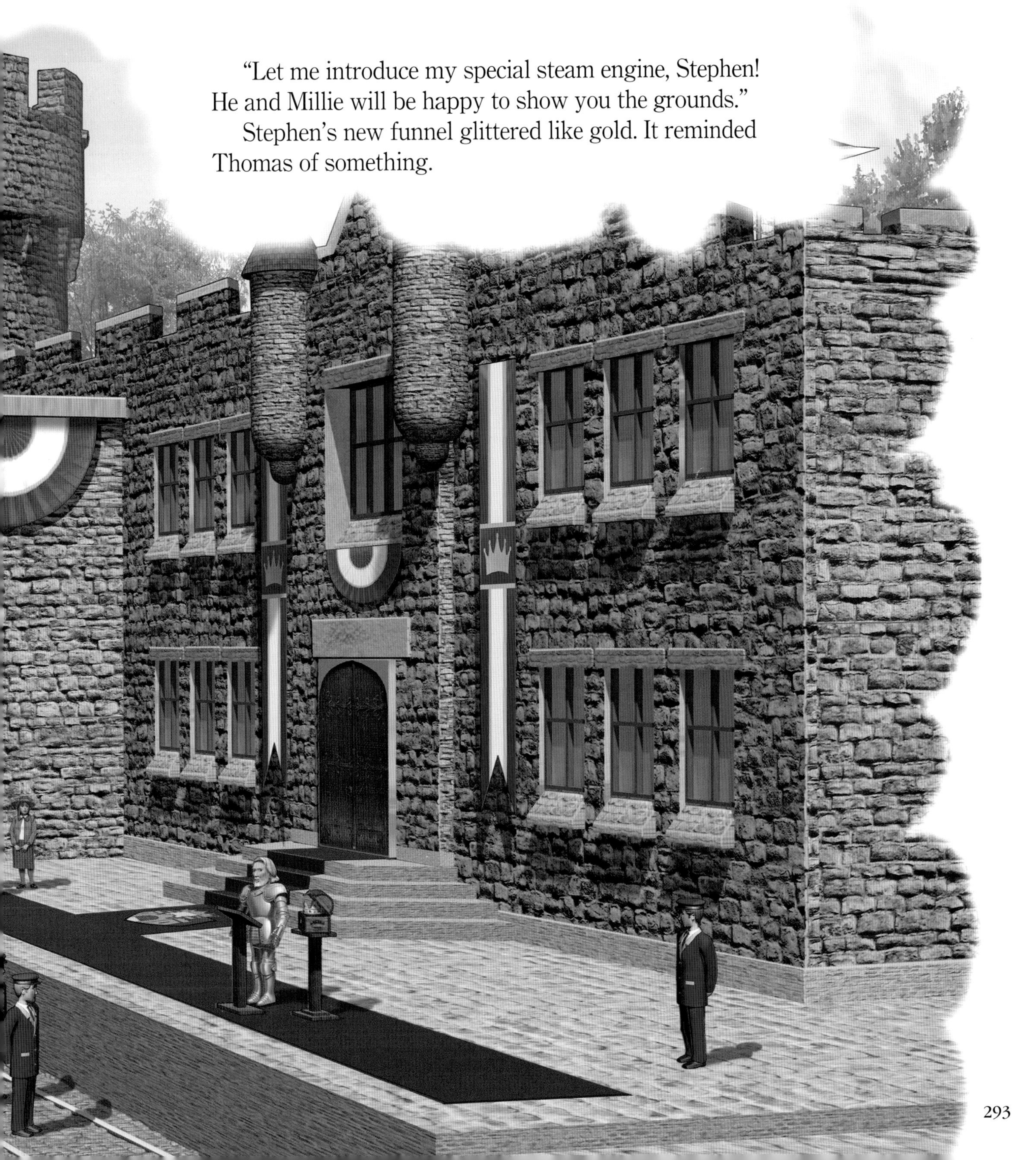

"Stephen found something I thought was lost forever," the earl said. "King Godred's long-lost crown!"

Thomas realized what Stephen's funnel looked like—a crown! The engines cheered for Stephen. He wasn't the fastest or the strongest, but he was Really Useful—and today he was a king!

# Risky Rails!

Based on The Railway Series by The Reverend W Awdry
Illustrated by Tommy Stubbs

BMQ
PETER SAM
4
RHENEAS
2
BMQ

**B**lue Mountain Quarry was a very busy place.

Owen moved equipment up and down the steep walls. Rusty shunted trucks of slate.

The quarry engines were smaller and lighter than the other engines and ran on special tracks.

Paxton, a visiting diesel, was impressed by the hardworking Narrow Gauge engines.

Suddenly, with a rumble, Blondin Bridge began to collapse! Rheneas saw the danger ahead and tried to stop. But his heavy load pushed him across the bridge.

Rheneas was safe! Everyone was relieved. Then they saw poor Paxton, half buried in stone. He wasn't hurt—but he needed some repairs.

Sir Topham Hatt asked Thomas to work in Paxton's place.

"I like working with my Narrow Gauge friends," he peeped. He chugged off to the quarry, where he was met with whistles of welcome.

The work at the quarry was hard, but Thomas enjoyed it. Suddenly, a small green engine darted out of a tunnel.

"Hello," Thomas peeped, but the engine rolled into another tunnel without answering.

The next morning, Thomas saw the little green engine again. "Who are you?" Thomas asked.

The little engine puffed off without answering. Thomas tried to follow.

"Go, Luke!" Skarloey cried as he and the other Narrow Gauge engines blocked Thomas.

“Who is Luke?” Thomas asked Skarloey. “Why does he run away?”

“He hides because long ago he did something very bad,” Skarloey said. “He’s afraid that if he’s found, he’ll be sent away from Sodor forever.”

Thomas promised to keep Luke’s secret.

Later, Thomas steamed off alone to think. "Don't worry, Luke," he said aloud. "I'll find a way to help you."

Someone was watching. . . .

The next day, Luke emerged from a tunnel and approached Thomas. "I'm sorry I hid from you," he said. "Will you be my friend?"

"I'd like that," Thomas replied.

Thomas and Luke worked together at the boulder drop.

Thomas asked Luke why he had to hide. They didn't notice that Paxton, who had returned to the quarry, was listening as Luke told his story.

“I came to the Island of Sodor by boat,” Luke began. “There was also a little yellow engine who spoke a strange language.”

“While I was being lifted off the boat, I bumped the yellow engine, and he went splashing into the sea.”

Victor's story about his journey to Sodor matched Luke's. But there was one big difference. "The chains holding my wheels were broken," he said. "That's why I slid into the sea when the green engine bumped me.

"When Cranky fished me out, I was in a terrible state."

"It was an accident!" peeped Thomas. "And you were repaired!"

"Yes," said Victor. "I chose to be painted red—a new color for my bright new life!"

"I have to tell Luke!" Thomas said.

"Is Luke the little green engine?" asked Victor.

"Yes," said Thomas. "And he needs your help."

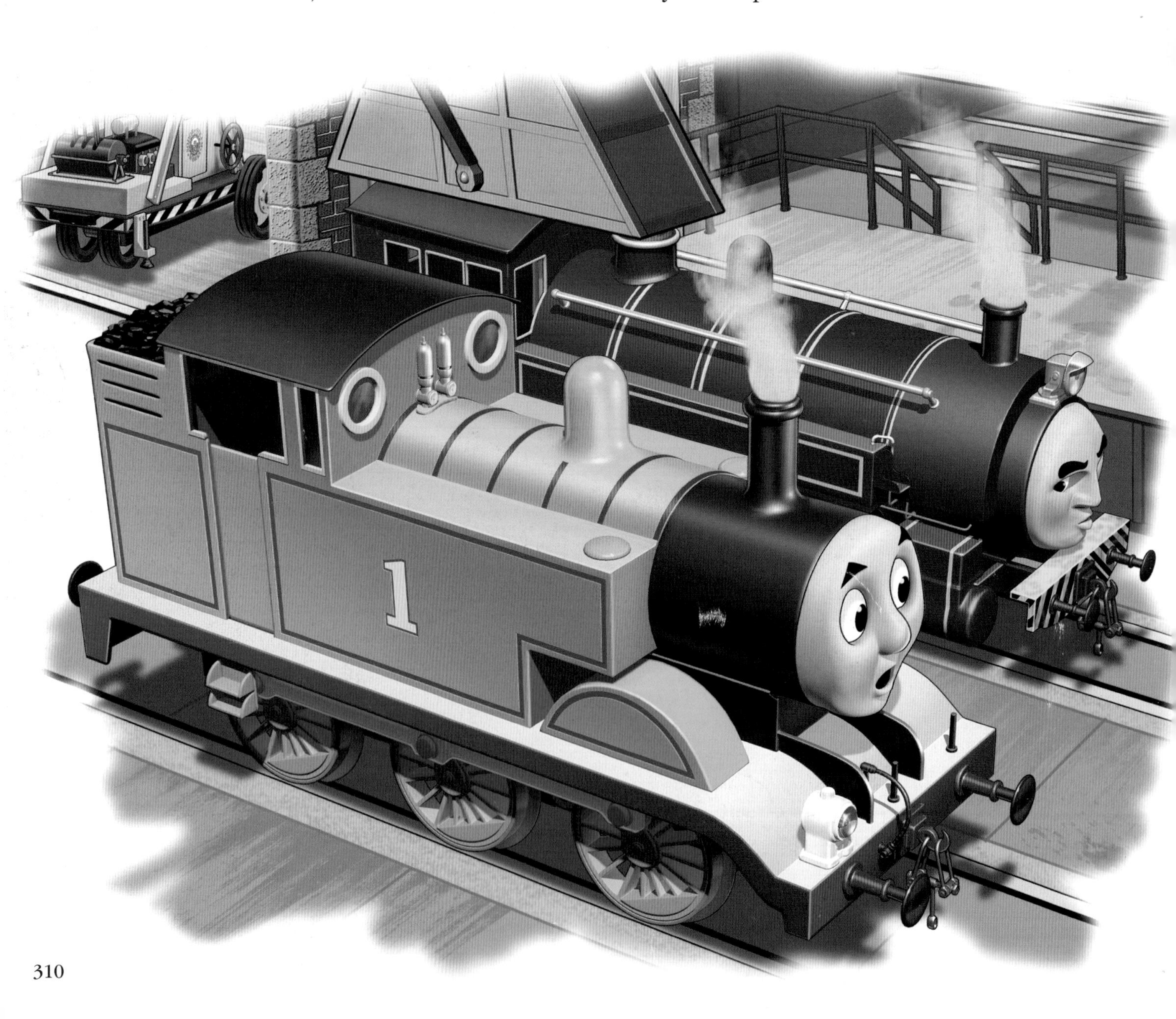

Later, Diesel and Paxton found Luke at the quarry. Luke rolled up the narrow-gauge tracks, where Thomas and the other engines couldn't follow.

"You can't hide now!" shouted Diesel. "Sir Topham Hatt is coming to kick you off Sodor! Even Thomas can't save you!"

"Yes I can," Thomas peeped as he sped into the quarry.

Rocky and Owen helped Thomas climb all the way up the quarry's walls.

But Thomas' wheels were too big for the narrow gauge tracks at the top. They jumped off the rails and Thomas rolled toward the edge of the cliff. "Help!" Thomas peeped.

Just then, Luke came around the bend.

“Watch out, Thomas!” cried Diesel. “He’s going to push you off! Just like he did to that yellow engine!”

“Don’t worry,” said Luke. “I’ll pull you back to Owen.” And slowly but surely, he pulled Thomas back toward the platform. Luke felt strong!

Luke got Thomas safely to Owen's platform, but the two engines weighed too much for Owen. The platform began to drop straight down!

"Cinders and ashes!" peeped Thomas.

Gears whined! Sparks flew! But Owen brought Thomas and Luke safely down.

Just then, Sir Topham Hatt arrived with Mr. Percival, the narrow gauge controller. They were confused and angry.

Then Victor steamed into the quarry.

"Luke, you didn't push me," he said. "It was an accident!"

Sir Topham Hatt was upset with Diesel. "You didn't find out what really happened," he said. "And the real story is what matters."

"Well done, Thomas," said Sir Topham Hatt. "Today is a happy day for Mr. Percival and his engines."

"Thomas has made it a happy day, Sir!" Luke said. "He's my hero—and my friend!"

Thomas and all his friends, new and old, whistled happily.